Praise

"Irreverent in a deliciously feminist way... Had me laughing out loud and wanting to share and discuss it with my closest girlfriends."

MARIA LEONARD OLSEN, AUTHOR OF *50 AFTER 50:REFRAMING THE NEXT CHAPTER OF YOUR LIFE*

"The ignored point of view of biblical women and all of us who followed. Bravo!"

MARY HAVERSTICK, AUTHOR OF *A WOMAN I KNOW*, FILM DIRECTOR OF *HOME* AND *TIPPING POINT PA*

"Her lens is a feminist one with God as an occasional interloper, protesting that he did not write a word of it... will make you, by turns, smile and shake your fist at the hijinks and misogyny that we are heir to."

PAULA MARANTZ COHEN, AUTHOR OF *OF HUMAN KINDNESS: WHAT SHAK ESPEARE TEACHES US ABOUT EMPATHY*

"Want to hear Eve's side of the Eden story? Or Bathsheba's view of David? And what really went on with Naomi and Ruth? Timely and thought provoking, sometimes anger-inducing, heart-breaking and humbling."

MERRY JONES, AUTHOR OF *THE WOMAN IN THE CUPBOARD*

"I wish Cordelia Biddle had been my Sunday-school teacher back when I was kid—church would have been a hell of a lot more fun."

LOUIS BAYARD, AUTHOR OF *THE WILDES*

About the Author

Cordelia Frances Biddle's novels focus on women's issues throughout history. Her early theatrical career inspires her to fully inhabit other lives and eras.

cordeliafrancesbiddle.net

LISTEN TO ME

The Women of the Bible Speak Out

CORDELIA FRANCES BIDDLE

www.vineleavespress.com

Listen to Me

Print Edition
ISBN: 978-3-98832-127-5
Published by Vine Leaves Press 2025

Cover design by Jessica Bell
Interior design by Amie McCracken

For my grandmothers

Eugenia Law Biddle

and

Mary Higgins Fenton

and

my mother

Frances Fenton Biddle

Three powerful women who taught me well.

Personae in Order of Appearance:

Eve – Supposedly the Earth's first woman

God – Also known in this work as TLGA ~ Nonbinary creator of the world. TLGA stands for "The Lord God Almighty." Needless to say, God detests the moniker.

Cain – Eve's firstborn son, a farmer

Abel – Cain's younger brother, a shepherd

Adam – Supposedly the Earth's first man

Lot's wife, later known as *Lottie* – first mentioned in Genesis 19 as a resident of Sodom

Moira – A contemporary Irish-American descendant of Eve

Ruth – A Moabite woman, appears in the book of Ruth, married to Naomi's son, Mahlon. Widowed, she subsequently marries Boaz

Naomi – Widow of Elimelech, returns with her daughter-in-law Ruth to her home country

Bathsheba – Wife of Uriah, widowed when Uriah is slain in battle, and then wed to King David

Les Trois Saintes Maries – Mary Magdalene, Mary Salome, Mary of Clopas

(Mentioned in brief)

Tamar – Appears in Genesis 38. Widow of Judah's eldest son, Er

Vashti – Queen of Persia, predecessor of Esther, appears in the book of Esther

Esther (historical) – Succeeds Vashti as Queen of Persia

Esther (contemporary) – Has a chance encounter with Moira

Deborah – Prophet and judge. The "Song of Deborah" appears in the book of Judges 5:2-31

Jael – Slayer of the enemy commander, Sisera. Appears in the book of Judges. The "Song of Deborah" extols her cunning and bravery

Delilah – Overcame Samson

PART ONE

Say What You Will

In which Eve sets the stage

Location and era of the reader's choice: a trendy bar in Soho, windswept mountaintop, opulent estate garden, derelict inner-city park, or...? Please also dress Eve accordingly. Or not.

Should you wish to time travel, let your imagination take flight.

Listen. I know the lies you spread about me. That I got us thrown out of that earthly paradise, dragged screaming from Versailles (insert any reviled queen or nation here), as well as being the downfall of many a good man, but, honestly, who are you kidding?

Wasn't old Adam (young then) also to blame? Or, perhaps more culpable because I was in quest of knowledge and he was ... well, complacent. If a snake could speak and reveal where and how you might attain wisdom, wouldn't you listen? Of course, you would.

I take it amiss that the world of men blames me, and that they've taught their wives and daughters to do the same. Anyone want to shout, "alewife, harridan, shrew, trollop?" And let's not forget "slut and ho" while you're at it. Go ahead; be my guest. But don't direct those cultish tirades at me.

Why does no one speak up for honest Eve? The kindest thing you say is that I was "beguiled," which means you think me stupid. I will not attack your intelligence, but I believe you have been manipulated and perhaps willingly so.

Consider that scarlet letter devilry, roasting witches (almost always "she"), female circumcision, the inane but menacing proverb about deceased virgins leading apes in hell. Could that be an invitation to rape? (I'm *not* asking for a friend.) Why, oh why, do we accept such revolting abasement? Fundamentalists within every religion and political party are feasting on our bones.

Which brings me to that rib thing.

And I quote:

> "And Jehovah God caused a deep sleep to fall upon the man, and he slept; and He took one of his ribs, and closed up with flesh thereof: and the rib, which Jehovah God had taken from the man, made he a woman, and brought her unto the man. And the man said, This is now bone of my bones and flesh of my flesh: she shall be called Woman, because she was taken out of Man."

Sound familiar? Yes, I realize there are abundant translations. I opted for the American Standard Version (ASV instead of flowery King James), but the gist is always the same. Some hocus pocus on God's part (I refuse to use the words Jehovah or LORD, which was a fav of King J) and I magically appear. Substitute an animal rib and the person I became would have been consumed along with a dash of special sauce ... But don't get me started on the choice of body part.

Then, and this is what really ticks me off, Adam calls me "Woman." Why? What's the "Wo" for? Unless, he meant "woe." And between you and me, I surmise that's exactly what he meant because spelling was never his forte.

Good in the sack, I'll give him that. And fun to be around. Especially when we were cavorting about in that swanky garden resort. But he admired brawn more than brains. Not his fault, given the circumstances of our existence. Rural doesn't even begin to describe the locale. Charming, I grant you, with that dense tree canopy and the heady aroma of those flowering shrubs, but hardly an intellectual's paradise. No, Adam wasn't created for a career in academia.

Woe, though, is precisely what misogynists throughout the ages have felt. A pox on them! And woe betide them, too.

But I'm getting ahead of myself, and ignoring the essentials like those stitched-together fig leaves (thanks to me and my homemaking skills), as well as the fatal enmity between my sons, Cain and Abel.

That was the kicker. My seminal moment of truth.

My sons. My dearest children. My sons.

Cain, my adored child. And Abel, also my adored child. How do I explain my anguish over the anger that bubbled forth in their innocent hearts? Two little boys who once loved one another. Two little boys who grew up to become angry men.

Try as I might, I can't discover how innocent sibling rivalry turned lethal. I blame myself. Of course, I do. I'm a mom, after all.

Although what I could have done differently eludes me. You mothers, aunts, sisters will understand. Women are familiar with woe—despite my mordant remarks regarding misogyny. Or, perhaps, those men were more prescient than they realized.

I shall leave you to ponder that question.

Adam also felt culpable. We didn't discuss the situation, but Cain's death drove a wedge between us. Trauma does that to couples. Look at the world around you. Look at your friends. And at yourselves.

God Weighs In

Scenic design of the reader's choice. God provides minimal suggestions.

Follow those proposals if you wish. God has weightier matters to consider.

Bear in mind that God is nonbinary. Eliminate ALL references to "He."

Do I bear responsibility for having helped create Abel and Cain? Could I have better built humanity's capacity for empathy? For morality? For compassion? Could I have prevented your addictive tendency to cruelty? Yes, if you believe that I created you. Even the agnostics among your kind who subscribe solely to the theory of evolution must ponder the question of my culpability.

I admit that I once urged you to slay your—"my" enemies. Urged you to obliterate anyone with differing viewpoints or deities. How can I answer those charges of incitement and fomentation, except in the affirmative? I was younger then and full of self-justifying righteousness. A poor defense, but true.

Genocide, pogroms, race extermination are now abhorrent to me. They should have been from the beginning of time, but, as I said, I was arrogant in those distant days. I aimed for perfection. I failed.

For those of you who believe that I had a human son, I pose a question: Didn't Christ preach love and inclusion, rather than hatred? Would Jesus have cradled an AR-15? I've seen the billboards in the US. I've read the bumper stickers. And I've heard your politicians and religious leaders throughout the globe spew repugnant speeches extolling sectarianism, injustice, and factionalism. Should the sacred be a tool for death? Should the sacred condone humiliation?

I digress. I must curb my impatience at you and at myself.

Where am I at this moment? I ask you to use your imaginations. Can you? Will you trust me? Not trust in God—which is rote—but trust me to reveal the truth?

I'm in a favorite retreat place, which is my kitchen. Don't picture the desert dusk and a wood fire overhung with clay pots, or sleek, stainless-steel appliances and granite-topped work islands and so forth. Don't picture angelic guests, either.

I'm alone. I like being alone.

And I'm doing the dishes. The thousands upon thousands of dirty dishes that your warring selves have bequeathed me.

I am scraping away mound after towering mound of rage and cruelty and violence, and I am weeping.

You don't think God weeps, do you? You believe I'm unsentimental. You are mistaken. With every fiber of my being, I ache for peace and reconciliation.

And hope.

That's Me: The Bad Boy

Might the location be an exclusive university? Or an oil-bespattered repair shop for aging, battered automobiles? Or a happy hour lounge in Vegas?

Please provide suitable clothing. If Cain critiques your options, let him.

I've gotten a really, really bad rap, and I'm pissed. Throughout millennia, Cain—that's me, in case you weren't paying attention—has been synonymous with evil. It's not my fault that I was driven to fratricide. Abel, that damn do-gooder, was to blame. And God. Or Jehovah or YHWH, or whatever name you prefer.

But we're never supposed to blame *Mr. High-and-Mighty-Fancy-Pants-Uber-Ideal*, are we? God the perfect, omnipotent sage and lover of humankind. Well, *He* didn't love me. Yeah, I know; that gender-fluid crap … But I don't buy into it. I repeat: Mr. Perfect didn't love me.

Ever.

No matter what I did or how many times I hallowed His name. Which, I assure you I did. And, if you noticed, I still use caps when referring to Him. Can't break old habits, can you?

It was all to naught, though. Adam and Eve's eldest kid was chump change to His Holiness. Why? Did He wish I'd never been born? Despise me from my birth? But wasn't a bouncy baby the deal? Offspring for the couple who were the light of His commanding eyes. Was it my name? Abel was, well, able: smiling, nice, helpful. Like a boy scout with all his goody-goody commendations.

I hear you say that I'm acting out, unable to let bygones be bygones, unable to forgive and forget, that I'm emotionally immature and unstable. That I should be on meds or tossed into a mad house or what have you. That I was probably always predisposed to violent and rash behavior, that my temper was ungovernable even as a kid, that I craved constant attention, etc. etc. etc. Oh, let's throw in narcissistic and sociopathic behavior while we're at it. Lack of empathy, too. Diabolical, maybe?

I ask you: Why do you loathe me? It's that vindictive Holy Roller's doing, isn't it? I wish I could blame you, jeer, throw stones and so forth, but you're dupes. You swallowed the Kool-Aid and did lots of other stupid shit. Self-castration for religious reasons, anyone? (Okay, after my time. Back in the day, we just sacrificed innocent beasts.) But you get my drift. You're blind. Seriously.

Sometimes, I wonder whether THE LORD GOD ALMIGHTY (full caps intentional) invented the escalating rivalry between me and my younger bro. Was it an experiment to see just how rotten humans could become? Look at the history of family dysfunction that has ensued over the eons:

Atreus slaughtering his nephews and feeding them to his sib—that would be the lads' loving dad, Thyestes. "Tasty stew, Atreus! Would love to get the recipe for my chef!" Thyestes wasn't such a stand-up guy though. Didn't he bed his own daughter? But that's merely incest not cannibalism, and a lot of you don't raise an eyebrow at a little daddy lovin'.

And let's not forget the race issue. The "mark" TLGA placed on me that darkened my skin, resulting in the lunatic belief that all Black people are inherently and irredeemably wicked. You see where this nutso logic leads. Cain and none other is the cause of all the world's ills and cruelties. I would apologize to my Black sisters and brothers, but it's TLGA's fault, not mine. (Got that TL?)

"Wynken, Blynken, and Nod one night/ Sailed off in a wooden shoe ..."

Did your mom ever read that to you when you were a kid? Yeah, I know, 19th c. American poet, but let's overlook the timing issue. Seriously. Cuz this rhyming stuff's important to me.

I loved hearing it, loved Mom's fluty voice, loved the rhymes, loved feeling loved and cherished. The poet's name still resonates with me—Field, because that's what I did when I grew up. I was a farmer. But you know all about my choice of career.

I don't think Mom could ever have guessed that I would dwell in the God-damned land of Nod after Mr. High-and-Mighty punished me. And just between the two of us, Nod was and is a shit-hole. There's no settling down in that region. For a farmer that sucks.

"So shut your eyes while Mother sings
Of wonderful sights that be,
And you shall see the beautiful things
As you rock in the misty sea …"

I hate my life. I hate myself.

TLGA Responds

silence

Abel Is Able, or Is He?

What locale would the adored child wish to occupy?

Might it be a playground dotted with slides, swings and seesaws?

An amusement park full of smiling families?

Or is he alone in a sylvan spot where meditation and self-examination come easily?

As long as I can remember I revered my brother. Worship wouldn't be too strong a term, but in our family, we only use that word for TLGA, as some people say. I'm on more intimate terms though, so I simply say God, just like you might call a favorite relative by a nickname.

As a kid, Cain was everything I wasn't: handsome, resourceful, smart, funny, a terrific athlete, and, of course, older. Dad doted on him. I did, too. I desperately wanted to be Cain's duplicate.

Mom used to try to soothe me and say that I was perfect just as I was. But you know moms. They like to make you feel better. Bloodied elbows, battered knees, a black eye (Cain was a sling-shot master): it's all the same. Hugs and cuddles and you're back on your feet and on your way. As a youngster, I loved my mom. Don't get me wrong. But maybe she was a little over-indulgent. Maybe a little blind, too. She saw what she wanted to see, but don't we all?

Anyway … Cain and Dad were an all-exclusive duo: hunting, fishing, palling around and joking. All that macho stuff. Stouthearted if you want a more antiquated term. They formed their own little world. Mom and I weren't part of it. I'm not complaining. Or, maybe I am. Yes, I liked being a momma's boy, but I really, really, really wanted Dad to love me. Cain, too.

Didn't happen. I don't know why. Families are weird like that, aren't they? One kiddo is "in," the others "out." Was it because Mom and Dad were polar opposites? Dad was a crash-and-burn guy. Out hunting, he was fearless and fearsome. Domesticity wasn't his thing. Mom was a total homemaker. I know that's an unpopular sentiment nowadays. The 1950s Betty Crocker housewife. But that's the mom I grew up with.

Cooking, making sure the tree canopy covering our dwelling was secure, tending our few domesticated animals. I loved helping with those chores. Yeah, yeah, yeah … I know what you're gonna say.

Was I on my way to growing up as a pansy, a pufter, homo, light in the loafers or all those other obscenities you brandish in order to jeer at male homosexuality? Why do you persist in heterosexism? It's vile as well as stupid.

I happen to know for a fact that God isn't a guy or a gal. Does that make God misguided like some idiots sneer when referring to sexual orientation they have no business judging? Give me a break.

If I dressed in fig leaves or animal skins just like Mom's, did that make me weird? What about Cain who hated clothing cuz it interfered with his image of himself as a tough guy? Didn't that make him weirder? Who wants to get cold and wet? Not yours truly.

So … childhood.

Looking back, I don't think it was happy. I wanted it to be a nice time, cheerful, fun-filled, harmonious. Mom did, too. Which meant that we overlooked a lot. Cain's anger management issues, his bullying, his jealousy. But why was he jealous of me, you ask. I don't know. He had Dad all to himself. Did he resent Mom for loving me?

I haven't a clue, and probably never will.

Was that why I became a shepherd, moving around, solitary, close to my animals but no one else? I've thought about this long and hard (I'm not making a dirty joke here). Before I was murdered, obviously, and nearly every day since, and can never find an answer.

I miss my brother.

Correction: I miss the brother I wanted to have.

Adam Speaks

Do not envision a haughty portrait by Sir Joshua Reynolds, nor a stereotypical "noble savage" inhabiting all continents throughout time and now embalmed in imagination.

Like Eve, Adam is a living person. Now and always.

Look, I'm not perfect. Nobody is. Could I have been a better parent? I can't answer that. I didn't have a dad or mom, for that matter, to show me how. You all yammer about children growing up in single-parent homes or foster care or on the streets, and wring your hands and blame the absent family member, blame poverty, blame the prison system, blame all sorts of local and global injustices for the fact that kids go haywire. That they do drugs, shoot up elementary schools, attack synagogues and mosques and Bible study classes.

Following your logic: Could I have gotten Cain on track? No. I didn't know how parenting worked. God "created" me but wasn't my dad—or parental figure, if you prefer that term. No awkward hugs or gruff advice about sex. No bonding over sports or beers. No conversation, period.

I'm not angry. I didn't know any better. I was Adam. An adult, drifting along, fed, warm, protected from the elements.

Have you ever seen the Tarzan flicks or the TV shows? Yeah, I know the concept first appeared in book form, but I'm not a reader. I believe Eve mentioned my lack of educational credentials. Anyway, my favs were the Johnny Weissmuller flickers.

That's who I was. Who I was happy being. I didn't need Eve. Not really. Did Tarzan need Maureen O'Sullivan? Gorgeous actress, but only there for titillation, in my opinion.

I'm not criticizing Eve. She was a fun companion and definitely not only a sex object. But she didn't know how to be a parent either.

So, let's be real here. Maybe God should have provided a few pointers before starting that pregnancy thing. Or maybe I should have hightailed it the moment Maureen O'Sullivan winked at me.

Just kidding.

Eve wasn't into being coy. Just ask the snake.

Eve Alone

Who would you cast in this part?

Did I mention that I love to swim? Ocean, lake, river: I'm equally at home. Am I avoiding my sorrows by hoping they'll float away? Maybe. But maybe I'm simply returning to my basic nature and finding time to meditate. I talk to the waves, talk to birds gliding overhead, talk to bits of seaweed, talk to the occasional fish that swims close enough to engage with me. I am in my element.

At the moment, I'm standing on a beach. Place it where you will. Pacific Ocean, Atlantic; the Med, Red or North Sea; Adriatic, Indian Ocean. Any seaside that you've experienced and can envision.

It's chilly. The sun has just risen and the sky has turned a luminescent apricot color at the horizon. The sea is a flat silver hue, calm on the surface, but teeming with life beneath. I wish I could breathe underwater, wish I could veer and scoot and dive like the finned creatures that call this their habitat. In a moment, I'll plunge into the cold ocean, gasp from the shock, kick for all I'm worth in order to warm up a bit, then take off and glide through this liquid and salty wonderment. I'll bury my face in it, open my mouth. I will become another Eve. I'll have a different history, a different future.

Have you ever wondered why there are so many myths about mermaids but few about mermen? My theory is that we're comfortable within elements we can't control, that we appreciate the charm and potential danger of the abstruse. And men do not.

There's a Yeats' poem about a mermaid that I always return to. Don't bother asking yourself why I know Yeats.

Unstick yourself from sacred texts and the limits of causality and spatial travel as I have. History is useful for comparisons, but shouldn't be limiting. Ditto artwork that affixes me to finite places and eras.

I'm a fan of HD, too, and Ellen Bass and Mary Oliver, among others. Oh, and Lamartine.

At any rate, in Yeats' telling of the tale, the mermaid finds a "swimming lad," clasps him tight, zooms downward—forgetting, of course, that he can't breathe underwater. The last line concludes, "even lovers drown."

How does it feel to have your eldest son kill your youngest? Many of you have experience with accidental deaths: unsecured handguns, car crashes; those tragedies that might have been averted but were not. You always live with a sense of time being frozen, the second or hour or day when oversight or better planning might have changed the outcome. I'm sorry for you. I am. I know you will never heal.

But I'm talking about a decision to murder a sibling. A decision. Not happenstance. Maybe the act was a last-minute situation. Maybe Cain had reached a boiling point. Maybe he couldn't control his temper. Maybe inner demons got hold of him. All sorts of maybes, but they all add up to the same absolute. Cain decided to murder his brother.

I cry out to God. I ask for wisdom (that snake was absolutely worthless). I pull apart every choice I made, every word that might have been misconstrued, but I cannot unravel the core elements that engendered Cain's decision.

Of course, I blame myself. What mother would not?

Did I overlook early signs of bitter jealousy? Did I tell myself that the boys' roughhousing wasn't that rough? That Cain never intended to make Abel cry? That he regretted every hurt he inflicted on his smaller sib? That Abel's eventual distancing himself from the family unit, and disappearing for months at a time while shepherding his flock, was a normal part of growing up? That maybe Cain's close relationship to his father contributed to that choice? Did I, perhaps, blame Adam for a seeming lack of awareness?

I think I did. But maybe I never asked those questions. Maybe I simply accepted the status quo. Boys will be boys. Men become men.

I make no excuses for myself. I live with continuous guilt and oceans of regret, but I also understand that I didn't know any better. Adam was always something of an enigma, his motives and behaviors were facts I accepted. Man is man.

We wives, concubines, mistresses make do, don't we? We carry on. Make the beds, sweep the house. But often we do so at the risk of avoidance. It's easier to cook dinner than to search out core problems and work to heal them. Easier to pin our faith on hope no matter how tremulous.

Oh, my child. Oh, my children. What would I give to eradicate your pain! Cain's tortured longings and Abel's rejected love. What would I give to reunite you in joy and hope. Everything. I would give up my life.

God Considers

Might you opt for a musical accompaniment? Might God play it?

Why did I favor Abel? Why, when Cain made as many sacrifices to me as his brother? And why did I desire sacrifices? I no longer do, but back then I did, much to my chagrin. It's a wonder that you humans have continued to worship me, but perhaps you did so out of fear. Perhaps, you do so still. I sincerely hope that's not the case, but I am uncertain.

I could attempt to justify my actions by saying that I was trying to teach you morality and respect for higher authorities, but, instead, I apologize. Cruelty is evil. I wish it didn't exist. I've tried to eradicate it, attempted throughout the centuries to instill reason and persuasion rather than barbarity, but then one of you starts singing, "Onward Christian soldiers, / Marching as to war ..." and I'm simply flummoxed.

I mean, come on! Medieval Italian Papal states battling other city states for control. Siena vs. Orvieto, for example, which meant that my supposed earthly and holy representative possessed a standing army and serious fortifications. To use a modern term: what the f—!

Can't I find a means to outwit and outmaneuver you?

Perhaps.

In time. Perhaps.

But I digress.

Being a tiller of the soil, Cain's presentations came from the bounty of the earth. Abel's were slaughtered creatures. Why did I prefer the latter? Did I feel they were more suitable to my lofty situation? Something living that was of intrinsic value to its owner? Blood smeared on an altar? Why? Didn't I also insist that Jacob sacrifice his own son? His beloved child! What was I thinking?

If I can't respond to those questions, I can hardly ask you to do so.

Cain brought me mere greenery for his sacrificial offerings: salad instead of roast lamb. Shouldn't I have been satisfied? Or did I believe there was a measure of contempt in his presentations? *That's good enough for the TLGA; I'm not wasting another cabbage or leek or wheat sheaf on this obeisance folderol.* Cain could be insouciant and cavalier. But he was faithful.

The fault was mine. I demanded too much. I was given to anger. "Smite" is the term you employ in scriptural passages. I did a lot of smiting.

Eve Recalls That Tragic Day

No author hints here. Let Eve carry you into the tale.

It was beautiful. The height of springtime, everything growing, everything abundant with new life. The scent of fresh grasses, leaves unfurling, and wildflowers mingled with the loamy aroma of the soil returning to fruition. The fabled Cedars of Lebanon in all their perfumed and majestic glory. It was dizzying, the blended odors: sharp, tangy, sweet, inviting.

And the colors, oh the colors! Have you ever seen moss lit like a neon-green sign, or yellows and golds that made you want to taste them as if they were composed of the finest butter? Every sense was mingled. Everywhere was birdsong. The entire Earth hummed with joy. I sang, too. As best I could. Warbling might be a better term. No one would have asked me to star as *Evita* in the Andrew Lloyd Webber musical, although the real Eva Peron was castigated as cunning and conniving and my spiritual offspring.

I'm deviating from the main story. It's hard to tell. I could punt and describe other family members—my daughters, whom religious texts conveniently ignore, determined to focus on the males, as if males alone can procreate and populate the planet. Now is not the time for me to rail against that inaccuracy and inherent prejudice, but I ask you to notice it. And to share my anger. And the anger of my daughters, then and throughout time.

On the date in question, Cain had invited Abel to walk the fields with him. I was delighted. The two hadn't communicated for months. There was always an excuse. One was too busy, one had too many disparate responsibilities. I recognized the responses as lies. Maybe convenient ones in order to maintain a masquerade of sibling affection, but deceit, nonetheless.

I considered suggesting a picnic and accompanying them, then decided I was being overly intrusive. A helicopter parent trying to bind together two grown children. I wouldn't have employed the term "helicopter parent" back then, nor would I have called adult males "children." In my heart, they were, but to the world they were self-determining men.

As you know, I didn't accompany them on their excursion. If I had, might we have avoided the cataclysm that befell us? Might my leavening influence have curtailed the violence, or might it only have delayed the inevitable? I wonder. Oh, I wonder.

Even now, I picture my sons strolling, chatting about this and that, maybe dredging up humorous childhood memories, maybe laughing about me or their dad. Or grousing. But happy. That's how I envisioned them as they trundled away. How I wanted to see them.

Please note that distinction. What we desire, and what is fact are often irredeemably different.

Forgive me. I must pause again.

~

What busywork task was I engaged in when Cain ran back alone? Hanging laundry out to dry, or preserving pickles ... something menial and mindless because my heart was too full of hope for a reconciliation to concentrate. Whatever it was, I'm sure I dropped the pillowcases in the dirt or let the Mason jars fall and shatter the second I spotted him.

His face was terrible, wretched and full of wrath. I knew in a single heartbeat that something terrible had happened to Abel, and my first instinct was to comfort his brother as I realized he'd blame himself. Hadn't they been on the verge of overcoming their differences?

I raced to his side. I didn't speak. Then I tried to take Cain into my arms.

He shook me off. His body was trembling and flushed with heat. He smelled of something too. Not maleness, but a goatish stench.

I forced myself to remain calm. We mothers do that, don't we? In times of crisis, we believe the world rests on our shoulders. Which, in fact, it does.

"Tell me," I remember saying, but Cain only snarled something and then howled in anguish.

I looked in the direction from which he had come. I don't know what I expected to see. Adam, carrying a wounded son home? Abel, limping forward, bloodied from having fallen down a cliff face? I stood straighter. Whatever accident had occurred, I understood that I was the sole person to rescue Abel.

"Stay here," I ordered. "Find your father. I'm going to your brother."

"Don't." That single word was a wail, but I remained insensate to its significance, and so again told him to look for Adam.

I started to stride away. Cain grabbed me. "Don't! Don't!"

I can't recall what happened next. Did I begin to run again? Did Cain forcibly restrain me? Did I fight back? All is a blur. One moment, sunshine on a lovely spring day, the next the field and our home seemed engulfed in spiraling clouds. Did it rain? Was there a surprising wind? I do remember that I shivered as though cold. Fear can produce that reaction.

Did I intuit the truth? I cannot say. Time was moving too quickly.

Have you ever heard God speak? Not as a whisper within your psyche, but as a booming voice? Something so loud that even the birds spiral upward in fear?

I will try to recall this exactly because I want to make sure the sequence is correct: what God shouted and what Cain yelled in return. Forgive my quaking voice. My mouth is too dry to swallow.

First, there was God bellowing, "Where is Abel, your brother?"

Cain trembled all over but stood his ground. Then he growled a furious response. "I have no idea. I'm not my brother's keeper."

"What have you done, you wretch? Your brother's blood drenches my earth."

For the first time, I noticed that Cain's hands were bloodied. He'd tried to hide them from me, I suppose. Or perhaps I was blinding myself to the truth. I reached for his shoulders, reached for his jaw and tried to gaze into his face. He raised his fists at me. Yes, there was blood. And hair, too. Abel's.

In that second, I knew he'd attacked his brother. I felt as if I'd been watching the assault unfold moment by monstrous moment. Cain had taken a rock, aimed it at the back of his brother's head, and then in a sudden and ferocious frenzy pummeled Abel until he was dead. Hadn't I always understood his propensity for violence? His utter lack of self-control? The anguish that impelled him?

"Dear child, what have you done?" My words must have been the merest whisper because my eldest didn't answer.

God's wrathful voice continued to cover the field. "From henceforth, you are cursed by the very soil that pools with your brother's blood. When you till the land, your work will be in vain. A fugitive you shall continue for all your days."

I was weeping by then. Crying and wishing and yearning that I could take us all backward in time, accompany them on their outing, point out the nesting egrets, the wildflowers, laugh and quiz them about the plants' names just as I had when they were young boys. It seemed impossible that I couldn't achieve that singular desire.

But I couldn't.

I took Cain's hands, purposely rubbing Abel's blood into my skin. Cain gazed at me. I shall never forget his appearance: horror, grief and fury mingled with utter desolation. I wanted to enfold him in my arms, rock him to and fro and sob together. But he turned away from me and stared toward God's voice. When he spoke, his breath caught in his lungs:

"My punishment is too great to bear. You cannot drive me away, or turn me into a detested fugitive. Let whoever finds me kill me."

"No" was the pitiless answer. "You will atone forever. A sevenfold vengeance shall be on anyone who dares kill you."

Then the wind rose; the sky crackled with lightning; giant hailstones descended, and Cain was struck by something and collapsed onto the ground screaming in pain.

"I have set a mark of my displeasure upon you, Cain, so that whoever finds you will not slay you. You must suffer for eternity."

Then my child, my dear child, rushed away shouting and swearing and wailing. I watched him run pell-mell, heedless of trees and the uneven ground. I stretched out my right hand but made no move to follow him. When he disappeared, I understood that I would never see him again.

After that, Adam set out to find Abel's battered body and bring it home. He didn't speak. Nor did I. Our eyes sought out each other's, but we didn't say a word.

Nor did God. There was not a single sound of solace or recrimination. I think the birds had not returned, for the skies were quiet.

The clouds still swirled, although their density had begun to subside allowing me to gaze across those once hopeful fields. I remember that my body shook and that a leaden hopelessness weighed down my shoulders and spine.

My boys were both gone. Both. My sons. Both gone from me forever.

Gone.

I cannot ... I still cannot ...

Cain

A solitary cell in a prison might seem too obvious a choice.

Would a private yacht cruising the Aegean seem preferable?

Or a C-suite in a global financial hub?

What objects and/or vistas do Cain's eyes rest upon as he speaks?

Do you wonder that I hate my life? Maybe I hate myself, too? When did my jealousy and anger at my brother begin? Say all you want about TLGA instigating my discontent with those unequal sacrifices on that holier-than-thou altar, but bitterness doesn't grow in a vacuum.

I can cast blame all I want, ignore any memories of my early cruelties, but the facts remain. I killed my brother. Killed a person who loved me. Killed the child who revered his eldest sibling. Killed innocence and my own self-respect. I killed hope, too.

I know—kids can be brutal to each other. They bully, tease, mock, punch when Mom's not looking, steal treats and toys and then feign innocence. Who me? I would NEVER ... (in full CAPS, of course)

I got away with all that mean-bro stuff. Looked wide-eyed with disbelief, disarming, as honest as the day is long. Deny, deny, deny, like they say.

But what happens when you've gotten away with murder your whole life? Was I pushing the envelope? Trying to see just how rotten I could be before someone called me on the carpet? Or did my nature creep further into decay with each unkind act: lording it over little Abel, jeering at Mom behind her back, lying? I did a lot of lying.

Or was I born mean?

But why? TLGA's initial experiment with the reproductive organs ... was I supposed to be a learning opportunity? People are routinely born with physical and mental challenges. ADHD, blind, crippled, deaf, dumb. I know those last four terms aren't in current usage, but they were back in the day. And, believe me, they weren't said lovingly. Remember "four eyes"? Remember "spaz"? "Retard"? "Village idiot"?

Okay: Moses' commandments. After my time, but I can assert I broke them long before ole Mose and TLGA hefted them down from the mountain top. "Thou shalt not kill?" C'mon. Didn't TLGA keep yammering about vengeance and smiting enemies? I will NOT discuss Moses' dictum against stealing, but you industrialists and banking execs, you greedy Bitcoin purveyors, slum lords, and sweat-shop owners, I suggest that maybe you need a little honesty about your usurious practices.

And what about that Jesus bunkum about loving your neighbor as you would yourself? A pretty picture, but what if you don't love yourself?

What if you never did? Ever.

How would you understand how that emotion works? Or would you feel envy for all who embrace one another? All the happy families hugging each other and taking selfies? All the dads cheering at little league games?

And would that envy, that feeling of being an outsider, the geek no one wants to sit next to in school, the kid everyone laughs at, the pimply boy who can't get a prom date … would that envy turn into rage at self and then spew out at others?

Beware the child with a heartsick soul.

Not Park Avenue: Mrs. Lot

But, in truth, yes Park Ave.

Or any city that reveres haute couture and the lifestyles it extols.

I'm Mrs. Lot of the above title. I'm jumping in to give Eve some necessary breathing room. Motherhood is wonderful but rarely easy, as I can attest. Anyone familiar with the book *The Park Avenue Face: Secrets and Tips from a Top Facial Plastic Surgeon for Flawless, Undetectable Procedures and Treatments* by Andrew Jacono, MD, FACS?

No? Yes? Neither Agree nor Disagree? This isn't a quiz, but I promise you that I, as Mr. Lot's spouse (who would be Lut for my Muslim besties), am NOT a devotee of facelifts, rhinoplasty, beauticians, spas, over-priced designer clothing and accessories and all the other fripperies that women of my income bracket are supposed to require.

Why did I receive this erroneous reputation? I am not vapid, not a sybarite; I don't "do lunch," don't idle away my days between fittings and manicures and massages. I am NOT a Park Avenue matron, nor the denizen of any exclusive, wealthy community or royal enclave where wives were and are regularly traded for younger, prettier versions. I'm looking at you, King Henry VIII. Also, Donald J Trumpery. Duke it out, you two, to see which is the more execrable.

So, why do you insist that my miserable fate was the result of gazing back yearningly at my homeland, Sodom? Why do you believe I wanted to live within its party-hearty streets and couldn't bear to leave? Where did those rumors start? With my dear hubby, *peut-être*? Didn't he manage to screw his own daughters?

My daughters, when you come to think of it. And I do. Often.

Listen, I have a lot (pun unintended) of friends. Some are gay, trans, bi, undecided. Gay sex is one-hundred percent acceptable in my world. Incest is another issue, but sex between partners of whatever gender is good. Laudable, in fact.

Raping angels, though? Seriously bad, don't you agree? Plus, they were our guests. Not that the overnight company issue should make a difference. Raping an angelic houseguest, wicked. Sodomizing (you didn't know the origin of the word?) devil-may-care friends, okay ... Hubby agreed with me re our visitors' safety. I mean, what decent host wouldn't?

BUT, and this is a big but, he offered our two unwed daughters (read: virgins) to the crowd clamoring to have group sex with our heaven-sent buddies. The guys passed on the girls, and kept shouting for those angel boys.

And this was the swell metropolis I wanted to remain in all the days of my life?

Let me explain.

The gory story appears in the book of Genesis. A caveat: who do you think penned those texts? I'll give you a hint; it wasn't women. Hence, the patriarchal slant of the tale.

Here's what happened. My telling of MY story.

Sodom and Gomorrah were dicey as well as pricy burgs. Think any big city before the AIDS epidemic. Think ancient Rome before the Visigoths descended. Venice prior to the Black Death. A happening spot like Studio 54 in Manhattan would have looked like play-school. Sex, drugs, and rock 'n roll. Fun times had by all. All the time. It had gotten out of hand, however.

So, these two supposedly random travelers show up, which is pretty much how angels always appear. Unexpected. I don't know what happens if you don't recognize them beneath the creased clothing and resolute air. Hubby, though, had gotten the angel vibe. He greeted them the minute they blew into town, insisted they take one of the guest rooms. They protested. He became adamant. I can attest to his impatience. He was not an easy mate.

We're all settled in for a pleasant evening when a mob surrounds the house demanding that we send our guests outside for group sex. I kid you not. Limoges plates, Baccarat crystal, Lalique, etc.: all those upmarket pieces start doing a jig on the damask tablecloth as the demands turn deafening. I can still hear the clamor: violent waves of noise, shrieks, screams. It was terrifying. Would those creeps have killed our guests after gang-raping them? My guess is yes.

Lot goes to the door, says, "Sorry, friends. No can do. These men are honored visitors. But ... you can have my two daughters who are still virgins."

Yes, he said that!

And, *yes,* he would have tossed those girls outside. Me, too, I guess, though as a mom I was damaged goods.

My daughters and I were too shocked to speak. Too frightened, as well. We huddled together, but there was no place that felt safe.

The mob continued to howl. People started pushing against the house, banged on the door, cursed Lot for being a foreigner. You know how this has played out in other cultures and other eras: Kristallnacht, that Chinese massacre in LA.

Hubby froze, then dithered. The house had been a big investment.

Our guests took action. They raced to the front door, tossed something at the thugs nearest the entrance, effectively blinding them and allowing us to escape. I don't know how they did it, or what chemical they used.

It wasn't tear gas. One minute we were inside and our home was shaking and starting to buckle from all that pounding, the next we were tearing through dark alleyways and out through the city gates.

As we fled, the angels warned us to hightail it to the mountains, but Lot kept hesitating and making excuses. He insisted on finding a nearby village. He was feeling his age, breathing hard, clearly panicky. The mountains were too far.

We continued to run toward this spot Lot had fixated on. The girls' fiancés were with us. I never had a chance to ask what they thought of their future father-in-law's efforts to traffic their intendeds. There wasn't time. We were fleeing for our lives.

Trying to catch my breath, I turned and looked back. If you think I did so out of regret, you're plain nuts. My daughters nearly gang-raped! Why would I miss Sodom? Or Gomorrah, for that matter?

Ask yourself what you would have done. You've got your girls with you, but are there other women who might be sacrificed to that vicious horde? Mutilation and gang-rape go hand in hand. Look at Ursula and the 11,000 virgins if you doubt me.

So, are there people you could help before you run for cover? Children fleeing abusive parents, fleeing sexual abuse from their fathers and uncles and neighbors?

I stopped, irresolute, gazed at my one-time home, now engulfed in flames. And was turned into a pillar of salt. I'm not kidding. Salt! Like a salt lick block for cattle! Not even something artisanal like *fleur de sel* or *asin tibouk*. Just a congealed mound of sodium chloride.

That's the Judeo-Christian version. In Islam, I'm so wicked that Lut deserts me on the city streets, and I'm killed by an avalanche of rocks. (Stoned to death, anyone?) One Hebrew tale explains the demise by sodium; I borrowed salt from a neighbor to make dinner for our guests. In so doing, I blew the angels' cover, i.e. I deserved my fate.

You know what it's like to be the target of rumors. Mean-girl gossip. Country club tittle-tatter. The "casting couch" if you're a successful thespian. You paste a smile on your face, square your shoulders, try to shake it off. But you can't. My condolences to you women victims. Any time you want to have a drink and kvetch, I'm available.

~

So ... There are my girls. Alone with dad, living in a cave up in the mountains. Mom has become a giant salt lick. I don't know what happened to their stalwart boyfriends, only that they'd skedaddled.

Now, we come to the incest part. Avert your eyes if you wish.

My two babies decided they needed to get pregnant and preserve this fine family line. They concluded that dear old Dad would do the honors. The stories you people keep harping upon have them getting Dad drunk and then sleeping with him. He's oh-so innocent and so shit-faced that he's completely unaware of the sordid situation. They're manipulative sluts.

Doesn't that negate absolutely everything we know about older men having sex with younger relatives? The girls are the seducers? They're the ones who groom the old farts? They're the ones in control?! Give me a fucking break!

God Provides A Word Of Caution

Let me expound on the creation of sacred texts. I, God, am not the author. Lot's mate already explained that fact, but I need to make certain you were paying attention. I didn't pen a single word. Nor did a journalist interview me, or a biographer spend years eliciting my thoughts on the mighty and mundane.

Ordinary men crafted those narratives. Perhaps, they didn't consider themselves ordinary. Perhaps, they believed they were exceptional because they could read and write and thought that celibacy and self-flagellation proved how pious they were. Personally ... No, never mind.

A brief history lesson. I trust that you're familiar with the First Council of Nicaea, which was a gathering of hundreds of bishops arguing about doctrinal choices and canon law. No woman was among that august group. Why?

I'm not saying these men were bad, although they did a lot of infighting over minutia, "full clerical privileges," and the wording in the Nicene Creed. I'm only asking why they didn't invite women to join them. Why they decided against including an equal number of church "mothers" as well as "fathers."

You weren't around when Constantine assembled the dressy ecumenical cohort, so I assume you're pondering the same fundamental question as I am.

On the other hand, if you're a fundamentalist of any religious belief, you're probably saying, "Damn right! Women have no right to govern institutions. Or their households. Or their bodies."

If I sound angry, I am. Perhaps, you've forgotten how incensed I can become. Perhaps, you've forgotten that I can and did demand justice, that I'm watching you at every moment.

I am not a cuddly grandma or doting grandpop. Yes, it would please me if you loved me, but it's unnecessary. Instead, I demand that you listen.

Women must be considered equal to men. Must be given equal opportunities and equal pay. Weren't Greek goddesses powerful? What about the Egyptians, Norse, Chinese, the females in the Rig Veda? The Hindu goddess, Kali?

So why the imbalance in the sexes? You scribes who penned the Judeo/Christian texts: What did you have against women? Look at the havoc you created.

I hold you so-called holy folk responsible. You use the cloak of religion to justify your cruelties, your wickedness, your fraudulence and insignificance. And incest, too. Your hearts are full of dust.

TIME OUT

Moira

No, she doesn't feature as a major scriptural player.

Let her twenty-first century pragmatism and honesty guide you.

I'm one of Eve's countless daughters. Not an important person. Just your average twenty-first century, white, middle-class female—that is to say, privileged. I live in the United States and teach middle-grade English in a public school, a career I love, but which comes with its share of challenges, as all jobs do. I'm devoted to my students from the gifted to the "prove-it-to-me" to the seemingly blasé. I also understand that they yearn for connections and guidance. I aim to provide both, along with lessons in literature and narrative form and development. Oh, and I *never* critique their unique voices as writers. Nor do I try to change them. The US of A may consider itself a homogenous nation, but it's not, is it? We come from every nation and embrace an amazingly diverse array of cultures. At least, that's the ideal, isn't it?

It's my ideal, at any rate. I hope it's yours. Banned books and "don't-say-gay" and all that racist, sexist cruel cant should have no place in our supposedly enlightened twenty-first century America.

But let me jump ahead.

Given my career choice, I may be overly sensitive to attention spans, but this tale is important to me. I can't control God's rants, so you'll just have to deal. But please let me know if you need a breather.

Do I see a raised hand back there?

Thank you for speaking up. Candor is important and asking questions is absolutely great! Well done, you!

Okay, then. Let's take this a little slower.

~

My story while we're hitting pause. I'm Irish-American. Note that I use two nationalities. One of my colleagues is Pakistani-American; another Brazilian-American. Or "American-Brazilian," as she says.

My mother's family came from the old country. They lived in Vermont, but their hearts were back in the various counties where their ancestors were buried. Some came to America because of the potato famine, some later; all were escaping poverty. They found work in New England, built homes, sent their kids to school and always attended whatever Roman Catholic Church was nearby. I have a hunch that their faith was tinged with a good amount of superstition, but they were devout people.

One relative and her husband went west homesteading and lived in a sod house on a prairie. It was said that she turned her face east every morning and gazed with yearning toward her vanished childhood home. Perhaps the dry weather conditions contributed to her grief. We've always been a people more comfortable with rain and damp.

My grandmother could intuit future events. She also was an interpreter of dreams. She had three daughters and one son whom she idolized. The daughters lit out as soon as they could and turned their back on any form of faith. Then came me. Moira. Don't ask me if I liked my name when I was in grade school. You can probably guess the answer.

As a kid, I was religious, sometimes to the point of obsession. I was the only one in my immediate family who attended church regularly. While my mother cooked pancakes and my brother sprawled around in his pjs reading the comics, my father would don a coat (covering his bathrobe), drive me to church, leave me off near the entrance and return home.

And there I was. Eight or nine years old, walking into what I'd been told was God's home.

I could lose the quarter I'd been given for the collection plate, or indulge in bitter envy (I desperately wanted to be a chorister wearing a long robe and admired by all), but God never failed to startle me out of my petty thoughts. I'd watch a sliver of sunlight emblazon the empty pew beside me, or hear the hymn billow up through the incense's blue smoke, and God would sit with me in that moment: my comforter, my guide, my perfect parent whose love wasn't contingent upon A grades or etiquette.

I admit that when I returned home to the smells of sausage and maple syrup, I felt infinitely superior to my earthly family. God didn't spend time with them because God had been perched beside me—in church. It's a wonder my parents put up with my gall. Needless to say, my brother did not.

This was during my self-styled "saint" stage. During our annual visits to my grandmother, I became steeped in the lives of the saints. I thought that if I were very, very good I might be permitted to join them. The flaw in the plan emerged when I became a teenager. Saints, I finally understood, not only have to be virtuous *all the time*; they must be DEAD. Don't ask if I was disappointed in having my hopes squashed. I'm sure you know the answer.

~

Okay, then. Now that I've shared some of my story, are we ready to move forward? Or do you want a bit more time to think and ask questions? Everything's on the table. No wrong theories or concepts. Let your imaginations go wild.

Yes, ruminate is a terrific word for this exercise. Also ponder. Contemplate. Speculate.

Now, who's going to volunteer and tell us about aliens because that's the story that's next up. No, not the type of beings found in speculative fiction.

I ask you to remember that these modern-day aliens are real people, many (if not most) of whom have been historically excluded because of their skin color or ethnicity or religious beliefs or sexual orientation.

Let us put an end to those vile practices.

PART TWO

An Alien Named Ruth

The title speaks for itself. Ruth's is a famous tale of triumph despite adversity. Or was it merely acceptance? Perhaps an impossible situation made tolerable?

When you consider locale and scenic elements, I ask you to take on Ruth's persona.

Before there were orations and marches promoting women's suffrage; before there were prison terms for suffragists; long before there was the issue of whether Black women could vote, I, Ruth, brown-skinned, a Moabite, made a life-altering decision. In the company of Naomi, my mother-in-law, I moved out of my comfort zone and accompanied her to her home country of the kingdom of Judah.

For those of you who have visited present-day Jordan, you know it's a beautiful place, and that what might at first appear arid—those treeless and dramatically sculptured limestone hills—are, in fact, fertile. In springtime, the greens of growing grains are incandescent.

The northern mountains are scented with junipers, cypress and wild olives. The aroma is clear and fine and energizing as all Earth's most pristine perfumes are. The desert areas have their own purity. When I lived there, oryx were plentiful. They're gone now, due to hunting—some legal, some not, because the oryx have magnificent and valuable horns. I understand that other species of gazelles and deer are also threatened. This is tragic, but I shall not dwell on the mistakes of the present era, for I have a vital story to tell.

It's the strong link between two women, and how we came to support and embolden one another.

The tale is well known to some of you, less familiar to others. In a nutshell: Naomi and her spouse and two sons moved to my homeland during a devastating drought in their own country. They put down roots. Naomi was happy, but like many transplants, yearned for her native land.

Her husband died. Her sons married local girls, as we were called—one becoming my husband whom I adored. Believe me when I say that we were incredibly happy. He was my beloved. I was his. And Naomi was always a welcome and honored guest in our home.

Then my husband and brother-in-law also died. Grief consumed the three of us women until Naomi realized it was time for a fresh start. With her sons and mate gone, her childhood home was calling her, as it does to all people who are getting on in years. It might be a village on the coast of Brittany when you've dwelt in

Paris for decades, or a Scottish island accessible only by boat: a place that has formed your heart and mind. You must return before you die.

Naomi said fond farewells to us, her daughters-in-law, but I couldn't sever our relationship. I don't know why I felt compelled to travel with her and desert my ancestral home, but I did. Maybe Naomi reminded me of my dearest mate and being with her was better than a loveless, childless widowhood. If I had remained in my homeland, I would have mourned the loss of the older woman who had become my friend and confidante. My sister-in-law wept but returned to her own people.

Naomi and I set off. Immigrants, political refugees and asylum seekers have made this gut-wrenching decision countless times, journeying in overcrowded and dangerous boats, in equally cramped trains and planes and battered vans with bald tires. Fear drives them. Fear heightens the senses as they race toward the unknown and pray that they'll find employment, shelter, a place that will welcome and comfort them. Above all, safety.

Hope impelled us. Naomi seemed to grow younger as we traveled. Picture yourselves as if you were accompanying an aunt or mother or long-time family friend on that precious journey home. You wander through the airport shops, buy silly souvenirs and overpriced gifts that make you both smile. You talk incessantly, excitement and anxiety motivating you. This is such a momentous step!

Then you stare down through the plane's windows as the pilot begins the descent. You can see her homeland, the green of a field glinting in the early morning sun, a river catching the quicksilver light, a few cars starting a daily commute. You squeeze her hand, say, "Almost there" while you wonder whether the place will live up to her memories.

In my case, I knew there was no turning back. No return flight. No TGV to the Gare du Nord.

We quickly settled in. Of course, we did. Naomi was always ultra-organized. Plus, her husband's relatives were still there. Distant, but kin, nonetheless. I made the best of it, looked cheerful and chipper, thanked everyone and tried to remind myself that Naomi had once been in my position, a foreigner speaking with a strange accent: uncertain, unsettled, afraid.

John Keats' poem "Ode To A Nightingale" mentions me. Two lines describe the emotional turbulence I experienced: "Through the sad heart of Ruth, when, sick for home, / She stood in tears amid the alien corn."

That was me. Sick for home, sick with memories of happier times and sometimes quietly in tears. I'm sure the same can be said of millions of other refuges and émigrés.

Naomi understood this. We were then living a pretty meager existence. I found what seasonal work I could in order to support us both. Naomi took on the domestic duties. In the evenings, we gabbed and gabbed. I heard stories she'd never shared before.

While she was reliving her youth within those tales, I accompanied her through time. We were comfortable within this cocoon of womanhood.

~

The man's name was Boaz.

I hear you saying, "Oh, there's always a man at the back of this, isn't there?" But bear in mind the era. Or, no, don't. Having the right to vote and maintain your own financial independence doesn't make most of us women any more powerful than we were back in the day. Look at the glass ceiling if you doubt me.

Naomi understood that my position within the community was precarious. Despite our obvious bond, I was still an outsider. Bluntly put, her death might make my life untenable.

In order to ensure my safety—and in all honesty, provide comfort in her declining years, she arranged for me to meet Boaz. Offloading goods in a warehouse, reaping grain, serving cocktails under the auspices of an exclusive catering company, the circumstances are the same: an attractive young woman, a wealthy older man. He was one of her most respected and respectable relatives, a perfect choice as far as Naomi was concerned.

In the scriptural retelling of the story (and PS I get my own book, not just a mention in Keats' ode), Naomi tells me to gussy myself up, sneak into Boaz's room after he's asleep, uncover his feet and lie there. I'm sure you're all wondering about the foot fetish thing. Translate another body part and you've got the story.

And I got Boaz.

Was I happy being his wife? That's a difficult question. I was safe. Naomi was safe. We had food in abundance and a comfortable home. I no longer worried about employment. Naomi could leave the cooking and cleaning to someone else, which she did. I smiled to see her lazing away her afternoons.

Remember, though, that I'd been married before. To a young man whose body had seemed more than lovely to me: muscled but sensuous, too. His skin emitted an aroma that thrilled me. When we kissed, I wanted to stop everything we were doing and make love there and then. He was the more reasonable of the two of us. He'd say, "Let's wait till we get home." I would have had sex at any time and in any place.

Boaz was not that man. He was old. Considerate, yes, but old. He smelled of age. Sex was perfunctory or nonexistent. I took no pleasure in it.

I was safe, though, and I needed to remember that fact continually. Love is fleeting, I'd tell myself. Be grateful for what you had. Not everyone is as fortunate. A love of a lifetime is a gift. Concentrate on that gift. I wasn't always successful with my assurances.

When Boaz and I had a son, Naomi was ecstatic, and became the most doting of grandmothers. We called him Obed.

She adored him. Her life had come full circle. Neighbors sometimes called him Naomi's child. Boaz gave her all the honor she was due as a revered older relative. She flourished, which is what you most desire for the women you love.

Sometimes, I thought that she and Boaz would have made the better couple. But no matter. Without me, the boy wouldn't have been born.

Eventually, Obed had a son called Jesse and a grandson named David—whom you all know.

So, I'm the great grandma of a king. Me, the person who once was despised as an alien, a nothing, the Hispanic hotel maid struggling to survive on minimum wage, the abhorred émigré bus passenger transported from Texas to Cape Cod, the lonely traveler with a broken heart.

I'm Not Mrs. Barrett

Ah, Bathsheba...

Readers: put out of your minds those pornographic depictions of David's "consort." She was NOT a model in a girlie magazine, nor did she pose for the artists who reimagined her tale. Every one of those provocative paintings would have infuriated her.

Please ponder her story prior to providing costume and setting.

I'm up next. And I'm not asking for love or pity or guilt. I just want to get the story straight. I'm Bathsheba, King David's illicit squeeze. Yes, that David who was Ruth's grandson. I know she wants to overlook the fact that her famous heir spent time lusting after the wife of one of his trusted military commanders, but she can't. Ever. Ruth is a pragmatist, a trait I have always lacked.

A poem by Rudyard Kipling, entitled "The Story of Uriah" will provide the gist of my tale. Ruth chose Keats; Eve opted for Yeats; I'm giving you Rudyard.

Yes, I can hear you complaining that Kipling was an Imperialist and racist, but he also wrote movingly about the common soldiers that the British Empire used as cannon fodder. So, sue me if you disagree with my choice. I've been through worse. Believe me.

Here goes. FYI, Jack B. is a stand-in for my husband, Uriah. Kipling wasn't kind to me, but he couldn't fathom that I had no option but to acquiesce to David's demands.

Ladies? Do I have your attention?

"Jack Barrett went to Quetta
Because they told him to.
He left his wife at Simla
On three-fourths his monthly screw.
Jack Barrett died at Quetta
Ere the next month's pay he drew.

Jack Barrett went to Quetta.
He didn't understand
The reason of his transfer
From the pleasant mountain-land.
The season was September,
And it killed him out of hand.

Jack Barrett went to Quetta
And there gave up the ghost,
Attempting two men's duty
In that very healthy post;

And Mrs. Barrett mourned for him
Five lively months at most.

Jack Barrett's bones at Quetta
Enjoy profound repose;
But I shouldn't be astonished
If now his spirit knows
The reason of his transfer
From the Himalayan snows.

And, when the Last Great Bugle Call
Adown the Hurnai throbs,
And the last grim joke is entered
In the big black Book of Jobs.
And Quetta graveyards give again
Their victims to the air,
I shouldn't like to be the man
Who sent Jack Barrett there."

Okay, here's what happened. Fair warning. Lust, sex, and felonious behavior. Uriah wasn't transferred to another posting. He was betrayed. I was, too.

It was springtime and the weather was hot. Uriah was away with other members of his unit. (No pun intended. Or perhaps, it is.) I've always like double entendres, and I'll admit to feeling edgy with the entire army out of town besieging some city or other. The king loved his wars. He even conquered Moab, the homeland of his great grandmamma, but that's another story.

Jerusalem was quiet, stagnant and boring without the troops. All of us army wives experienced various degrees of anxiety. Even of abandonment. We met up regularly, played mah-jongg and what have you, but we missed our husbands (and having sex, of course), missed lively dinner parties, dances at the officers' club, getting gussied up, having our hair and nails done, shopping and showing off our latest purchases. Book clubs didn't fill the void. To say nothing of tennis or golf. The weather didn't help. No one had any energy. We wanted our men back in our arms and beds.

Why the king stayed in town remains a mystery. Shouldn't he have been off parading around with his armed forces? Being a big shot? I have my hunches as to his motives, but that's all they are. They're not admirable hunches, however. I won't use the words indolent or timorous, but both niggled at my brain. This was our nation's guiding light?

I'm not saying that I prefer a man in uniform, which you might infer since I was married to the brass, but I do revere heroic behavior. An officer and a gentleman. Semper Fidelis. Conspicuous Gallantry. *Croix de Guerre.* My husband was that kind of person. Noble. Forthright. Selfless.

Our apartment complex was fairly near the palace. As I mentioned, it was beastly hot. I'd gone outside to sluice off and try to catch a breeze. None of us girls were wearing much. With the guys gone, any pretense at formality was gone, too.

So... the king was prowling around on the roof of his fancy castle. Was he spying on us semi-clad gals? Deciding whether to send out for pizza or order up a little something on the side? You know that kids' ditty that refers to King David's "many, many lady friends and many, many wives ..."

All I can tell you is that the next thing you know his limo arrives and I'm whisked away. Before you can say Jack Robinson (or Barrett), I'm in the king's gold-plated bedroom. Champagne chilling in an ice bucket, the king in a silk dressing gown, embroidered with his initials encircled by a crown.

He poured me a glass of bubbly. I nodded politely, but hesitated. I had a feeling he was making a pass at me, but I tried being pragmatic, which, as you know, isn't my strong suit. I told myself that he respected my husband, that he needed him and therefore would never overstep the bonds of appropriate behavior. I reasoned that my visit was in Uriah's best interests. Maybe the king was considering a promotion and wanted to get my thoughts on the matter. Get my approval, perhaps.

I was wrong.

We know all about Spanish fly now, don't we? Bill Cosby and his repulsive jests. Lawsuits. Rock stars, et al. And before those cretins, there was the Marquis de Sade lacing the drinks of his amours with cantharidin, which is the same thing. The stuff was supposed to set the women afire. It did—with excruciating abdominal pain. Not the best aphrodisiac.

I was clueless, though. I accepted the flute of Champagne, smiled in deferential gratitude, promised myself all would be well.

When I came to, I was sprawled in the bed, naked, bruised, miserable. The king told me I was beautiful, which made me want to vomit. Maybe I did. My head was spinning; the room was spinning. I panted, but the nausea wouldn't cease.

Then one of his servants whom I'd never seen, a dark-haired woman with eyes circled in kohl, helped me climb back into my clothes. I was trembling all over. She assured me the "Champagne" would wear off soon.

After that, I was carted home in the royal limo.

~

That afternoon's enforced siesta got me pregnant.

Don't ask me how I felt because you already know. All you #MeToo gals. All the victims of "seduction" as it's referred to in Eng. Lit. Such a genteel word for a criminal act!

I confronted the damn man. Gloves off, despite what he might or might not do in retaliation to my husband. I didn't care at that point, but I wasn't thinking clearly. And what do you think David did? No private stay at a resort-like clinic and a discreet surgical procedure. No attempts at hush money or gifts, which I never would have accepted. Never. I had the upper hand or so I believed. And I was full of wrath.

Then he brought my husband home.

Here I am harboring this horrible secret, but I'm also thrilled to see Uriah. I clung to him, covered him with kisses. How dearly I wanted to explain what had occurred! But I couldn't. Uriah would have attacked and probably killed David. Then he would have been slain in turn.

I had to keep silent.

The king had it all planned. Lonely, horny husband returns home, has sex with his wife who then becomes pregnant. Except that she already was.

There was a problem with this reasoning, however. Uriah was honest, a hero, an officer genuinely concerned with the well-being of his troops. He didn't deem it appropriate to have sex with me when his men were bivouacked in open fields and eating MREs.

"Let me sleep on the coach," he told me. "Better yet, outside. When the fighting ends, we'll have a real vacation, I promise. Paris. Rome. Anywhere you want to go."

The next day, David got him drunk, but Uriah clung to his principles. He came home from the palace but not to share our bed.

~

After three short days, my husband, my dear, dear mate was dispatched again. Our goodbyes were hurried and weird. I wondered if he could guess my secret. I won't call it infidelity because I was a victim. But I wondered. We were so very close, reading each other's thoughts, anticipating each other's words.

I had a terrible feeling I wouldn't see my man again. You know that bad luck superstition that warns you not to watch a loved one disappear from sight? You're supposed to turn away before they're gone. I'd always done that. Always. Smiled. Waved. Then spun on my heels and looked in the opposite direction.

This time I didn't. I wanted to call him back. Wanted to take him in my arms. I wanted to confess. Start a new life somewhere where that sleazy potentate couldn't find us. But the jeep was already in gear and backing out of the driveway. And that was that.

Not quite.

While I waited, pondering my future, my senses alive to apprehensions, forebodings, guilt and rage, real tragedy lurked.

When Uriah had driven to whatever city the army was in the midst of besieging, David sent a letter addressed to his superior officer. He ordered the man to put Uriah "in the forefront of the hottest battle, and retire from him, that he may be smitten, and die."

Those were KD's exact words.

And I had to marry him.

Marry the man who murdered my husband.

God Is Weary

"And it came to pass, at the return of the year, at the time when kings go out to battle..." I'm quoting a religious text that begins Bathsheba's story. What put that idea about seasons and their usages into your brains? I didn't. I REPEAT. I DID NOT WRITE ANY RELIGIOUS TEXTS.

For centuries, you've been abusing those words to explain David's presence in Jerusalem when his army was away fighting. Does that excuse his assault on Bathsheba and subsequent murder of her husband?

Listen to me. I'm enraged by his behavior. You people in positions of power will understand my frustration. You have a new hire, a PhD candidate, the child of a friend you've taken under your wing. You've greased the skids as I did with David, overlooked certain insufficiencies and too many excuses, because you dearly want this mentee to succeed. So, you keep encouraging; you manipulate wins. Be forewarned: Your enthusiasm can produce problems.

If you're familiar with Bernini's statue of young David before he fought Goliath, you will understand the person I wanted him to be. The person I trusted. Slingshot at the ready, jaw set, brow furrowed, expression steely. He's a young man on a mission to save the world.

"How the mighty have fallen!" David said that about Saul, his hero who committed suicide. The words were prescient. David could have been referring to himself after the Bathsheba debacle. Or I could have uttered them.

David's behavior regarding Bathsheba and Uriah was amoral and cruel (to say the least). I cannot forgive it. I've tried. Tried to remind myself that he subsequently suffered his own betrayal at the hands of his son, Absalom. But I wanted more from him.

I want more from all of you.

PART THREE

Eve, Ruth, Bathsheba Confer

You have free rein with setting, costume, casting, lighting design and scenic shifts here. The choice of music is also yours. Is there an old LP playing in the background? Or perhaps a favored playlist?

The women envision locales in which each is familiar. What is yours?

"What happened after he forced you to marry him, Bet?" Seated on the porch of an island beach house she rented for this reunion, Eve leans forward, studying Bathsheba, but deciding that a gesture of fondness or even pity might deprive her friend of the strength she's fighting to preserve.

Bathsheba doesn't speak. Neither does Ruth. Instead, they gaze out at the ocean, seeing the varying bodies of water each has known in other times: Sharm El-Sheikh and the Red Sea, Killiney and the Irish Sea, Zamboanga on the Sulu.

Eve watches her companions as they tunnel inward, journeying through cosmic spaces and remembering.

The jigsaw puzzle that the three began lies momentarily forgotten, spreading shards of incomprehensible attachments across the surface of a saggy card table. Bathsheba discovered the box sitting forlorn and dusty on a shelf. The image is of Botticelli's "Three Graces," a detail from his painting "La Primavera." She couldn't stop guffawing as she retrieved it. "That's us, ladies! Let's hope a previous renter didn't abscond with these gals' body parts!" The mound of pieces has seen only intermittent interest, but Bet still considers her discovery ironic and amusing.

Eve looks away from her friends and their current diversion. She also finds herself pondering the past. For a moment, the present vanishes and her gaze moves toward the ocean. Turbulent dark spots flash within the salt waves; schools of fish, she surmises.

She imagines swimming with them, letting them guide her in their fluid undulations. Bet and Ruth aren't devoted swimmers. They prefer the wide, breezy porch and a dip if it's warm enough. Eve's aware that Bet would have voted for a full-service, five-star resort for this gathering while Ruth loves empty desert spaces. Next time will find them in another spot. For now, though, it's her show. She repeats her question, pushing a little, but still gentle.

"I had a son who died in infancy. David considered it divine justice, which it probably was, but that didn't make my loss easier to bear. Losses, in the plural, I should add. Then eventually I gave birth to another boy. David named him Solomon. He inherited the throne. But you already know all that. Besides, haven't we discussed this ad nauseum?" She picks up a puzzle piece and puts it down without looking for a likely match.

"But you, Bet? I'm asking about how you fared, not David or Solomon or anyone else."

"What does it matter? I'm here. 'Sitting up and taking solids,' as they say."

Cynical and measured though the tone is, Eve hears fury within it. "We're talking about you, honey. Forget the others."

"I think …" Ruth's voice is soft, hesitant. Her fingers graze a cardboard depiction of diaphanous cloth, then move on. "I think I may be partly to blame."

Bet spins toward her. The wicker-work chair creaks. It's old, an antique of some kind that came with the rental property. The owner clearly sets store by it, but she finds it uncomfortable as well as overly dainty. Her sudden movement jostles the table, causing several puzzle pieces to cascade to the floor. "Why would that be?"

"Because my son … and grandson …"

"Oh, for pity's sake, Ruth! You're not responsible for the bad guys of this world. I said it before, and I'll say it again. I really need you to hear me, babe."

"But …"

"Look, you were young, a widow barely out of your teens. You lost your husband to natural causes. I'm not suggesting that's easier than what I endured because you obviously grieved. And doubtless still do. You loved the guy. Had fabulous chemistry. Loved to fuck as you're fond of reminding us. Not using that precise term, though. Then he died ... So, please use some of your famous pragmatism on this situation. Your grandson was his own person. His choices weren't your fault. Besides, you never even met the man. How could your personality have any bearing on his?"

"But Boaz—"

"One rapist to another, is that what you're saying?"

"I wasn't—"

"Right."

"Marrying him was my choice."

"Oh, honey, spare me. You're too optimistic for your own good. Too optimistic for me, too." She laughs, the sound harsh. "Sorry to interject current ideological infighting. Or maybe I'm not." She tosses herself backwards in the chair, her multiple gold bangles clanging. "#MeToo!"

Eve stands. It's not that she's stiff from sitting, although the three have been perched in the same positions for what seems a long time. Movement, however, is the only recourse she believes can alter the mood, but then she's always been more physically active than they.

"Lunch, ladies?"

Ruth smiles. Bet also smiles, but her aspect has a bitterness that she can't conceal. Then, too, superior accommodations might have assuaged her anger. Having lived in her nation's capital, she's accustomed to a more exclusive realm than her friends. Better cuisine and richer garments. Today's choice is Balenciaga. She has two suitcases full of similar outfits upstairs: each of which will probably remain unworn in this rustic locale. Although she understands the roots of her dissatisfaction, altering her reactions is another matter. She almost feels like sweeping the puzzle from the table; instead, she flicks away a feathery dandelion puff, takes a steadying breath and grimaces.

Looking down at the dour expression, Eve grins and shakes her head. "I know what you're thinking, darlin'. Tuna melt, again."

"Sounds perfect." Ruth turns toward the ocean vista, her face unexpectedly mournful. "What a heavenly view. I'm so grateful that we can spend time together. And in whatever spot we choose."

Bet rolls her eyes. "Aren't you afraid of eating your aquatic siblings, Evie?"

"Not if you're not."

"I fear nothing."

"Good. That's an excellent emotional place to be. Talking it out like this helps. Now, if you two set the table ..." Leaving her friends, Eve crosses the porch toward the door.

Her focus still seaward, Ruth remains silent for a minute or two. "You know, Bet, I've been thinking ... Wouldn't it be fun to include the other gals for our next reunion? It's not that I don't love being alone with you two ..."

"Don't think I'd use the word 'fun,' sweetie."

"Well, you know what I mean ... cathartic ... or whatever it is that Evie's always after."

Bet's lips form a genuine smile as she studies Ruth's earnest expression. "You really are a sweetheart, babe. I hope you understand that. Kind. Good. Pure of heart. Shirley Temple in grown-up form. Okay. The other gals. Lottie, et al ... I'm in. Why not? Maybe, we can even arrange to Zoom with them later today or tomorrow. Or FaceTime, or whatever. Eve's certain to have current contact info."

"Oh, yes, let's! And next time, we gather in person."

"In a space this size? You've got to be kidding me. No way I'm sleeping on a foldout. Or an inflatable mattress. *And,* I'd rather have an original Botticelli to contemplate."

"Then we opt for another—"

Opening the door, Eve turns back toward her guests. "Ladies? The table?" Then she looks toward the water again, and her eyes lose their focus as if she's watching a different scene. She tilts her head, her heart roving into the distant past. Then she begins to sing:

"Wynken, Blynken, and Nod one night
Sailed off in a wooden shoe,

Sailed on a river of crystal light
Into a sea of dew.
'Where are you going, what do you wish?'
The old moon asked the three.
'We have come to fish for the herring fish
That live in this beautiful sea.'
The old moon laughed and he sang a song
As they rocked in the wooden shoe
And the wind that sped them all night long
Ruffled the waves of dew …
Now cast your nets wherever you wish
For never afeard are we …"

Eve bows her head. The screen door clangs shut behind her. "I can't. I just can't."

Les Trois Saintes Maries

As in the prior chapter, your scenic additions are welcomed and encouraged.

I'll continue because Evie's upstairs crying her heart out. Ruth's with her. I'm not much good at consoling, so I'm still on the porch. Needless to say, there've been no tuna melts. Not that I mind. Caviar and pâté de foie gras are more to my taste. And Veuve Clicquot, which, as you know, was my downfall.

I wish Eve didn't insist on us staying in homespun places like this. No decent takeout. No restaurant worth mentioning for miles. Just nature, nature, nature. And other reclusive folks who like communing with it. I realize that I shouldn't kvetch. Eve lived in a different environment than I did. That formed her personality. Also, she wants us to bare our souls and dig deep and ponder all that psychoanalytic crap. Thus, the motivation for this sequestered spot.

That doesn't make me love her any less. Or Ruthie. It's just that I'm, well, different from them. We all are, aren't we? And that's a good thing from my point of view.

The story I'm about to share is pretty weird, but bear with me. Tales about saints can stretch the limits of perceived truth. Not that I have anything against faith. It's just that I've never found it consoling but given my history that's probably understandable. Plus, the saint escapades happened waaaay after I appeared on the scene. That Messiah figure started it all. No saintly personages prior to his arrival. I wonder why that is. You're probably wondering, too. Happy to discuss later if you wish.

To continue: If you haven't heard of Les Trois Saintes Maries, well, now you have. In the French Camargue at the intersection of the Rhone River and Mediterranean is a charming Medieval town, Saintes-Maries-de-la-Mer. It's been engulfed within a seaside resort now with hotels and restaurants dotting the coastline. Inland are marshes where the famed red rice grows. I recommend it.

The town formerly centered on a church named for the three female saints. Not so much now, of course, because, well, religion whatever the persuasion, has lost some of its grip and grandeur. I would argue that we worship money and worldly goods instead, but that might seem heretical coming from the wife of King David.

The saints in question were Mary Magdalene, Mary Salome and Mary of Clopas. I'm sure you recognize the first name. In some stories, she's a sex worker, maybe also the Mary who anointed Jesus's feet, definitely a watcher at his tomb. Mary Salome was purportedly Jesus' aunty; Mary of Clopas was also present at the sepulcher for the man's miraculous resurrection. Don't bother to ask yourselves why no guys bothered to stick around. You know the answer.

I sense confusion. Wait a minute ... Aren't we talking about the south of France? What does that area have to do with ancient Judea? How did the ladies get there? Not on an El Al flight.

I knew you were smart.

Legend has it that the three hopped aboard a raft (maybe a small boat) and cruised across the Med, circumnavigating Italy, Sicily, Sardinia, and Corsica until they happened to make landfall in the very southernmost area of Provence. I would have chosen Cannes, but no matter.

It boggles the mind to consider: a. that lengthy and undoubtedly treacherous voyage and where they took on provisions and b. supposedly sane people believing that three residents of an ancient Roman colony would light out for France. Gaul, it would have been back then, but still under Roman rule. Was that a wise choice for followers of a person Rome had crucified?

I recognize that faith is faith, but shouldn't there be a modicum of actual fact upon which to base the tale? I have no beef with the three Marys. Either they made the voyage or they didn't. And Mary Magdalene, as one of the three who brought Christianity to France? Is there a subtext I'm missing? If—a big if—she was a sex worker, is there a wink and a nudge and an *Oh là là,* let's get those can-can girls doing their racy thing? I hope not, but I wonder. Hasn't Paris been considered a mecca (not the religious kind) of hedonism for centuries? Didn't the British refer to a condom as a "French letter?"

Excuse my flippant tone. Despite what I said about Eve being overly analytical, I'm looking for serious answers. She and Ruth get after me for being too jokey, but maybe it's my attempt at self-protection after waking up with a giant hangover and endless regret.

If this sounds like a pity-party, I guess it is. You see, I had no one to love. Ruth had Naomi, but I was alone. My son, Sol, I hear you murmuring, but do you honestly believe David would have entrusted him to me? Me, the easy lay, the fallen woman?

Yes, that baby thing was David's fault, but do you think he took responsibility? Or showed me respect or even tenderness?

I assume he was ashamed. But maybe he was merely bored. After my first son died, I became nothing but a womb. Then baby Sol was wrenched out of my arms, given to a wet nurse, and thereafter dispatched to nannies, teachers, tutors. When I saw him, our meetings were formal, supervised. He never thought of me as his mum.

Being wed to a rich and powerful man is a lonely, hellish life. How can you find a real friend, an honest shoulder to cry on? Everything you say is reported. Judged. Misconstrued. Everything you do is found lacking in some crucial manner as if you were too stupid to know better.

I was allowed to take walks in his gardens, swim in the pool, buy designer clothes but I had no autonomy. None. Eve understands this, but she wants me to acknowledge it. So, now I am.

You young women out there who think life will be ideal if you can just snag a well-heeled guy despite his age or peculiar predilections, don't do it. Run in the other direction as fast as you can, and if your parents complain tell them Bathsheba advised you.

Yes, my existence looked glitzy from the outside. Gobs of money, a lavish residence, hot and cold running servants, but I was a prisoner. With no child to hold.

The Upstairs Bedroom

Sit with Eve as she confronts her grief.

The room is filled with light. Too much, perhaps, for my eyes are swollen from crying. I didn't intend to fall apart in front of the others, but I did. Ruth provided as much solace as she could, but in the end, I simply wanted to be by myself and sink into my own void.

Why does this anguish never cease?

I no longer pray to God because I don't see the use. God can't restore Abel to life, can't bring Cain back to me, can't alter that terrible day—or the years leading up to it. What did I do wrong? I wish I could blame someone, but I cannot. Adam was as clueless regarding parenting as I. Our boys' fatal conflict wasn't his fault. I try to tell myself that it wasn't my responsibility, either, but every fiber of my being screams otherwise.

Where is Adam now, I wonder. Is he managing okay? Feigning a strength he doesn't feel? Showing the world a stiff upper lip. Hiding his pain? I hope not. I hope he has found someone to console and care for him. Maybe he's created another family. I think he was capable of doing that. Most men are, aren't they? Except for those who have been traumatized by war, and who never again know a peaceful night or quiet soul.

Adam never saw combat, though. Not like Bet's true love and true husband. So, I hope that wherever Adam is, he's at peace.

There are pink and coral-hued geraniums in front of the window. The rental owner arranged the clay pots on elevated white wicker stands. I should take them outside, for they should have more sun, but they're very pretty where they are. I wish I could commune with them, wish their cheerful natures could make me less sorrowful, but perhaps I'm mistaken as to their psyches. Maybe they regret being divided into individual planters; maybe their individual bodies miss the severed roots.

Oh, Cain. Oh, my son.

Ruthie Speaks Up

Do I hear you applauding her?

Of the three of us, I'm admittedly the most conventional. Bet and Evie insist that I'm probably too much of an optimist, as well, and I guess I am. But the personality trait has allowed me to carry on with my life. I take what good I can and when I can. I try to find hope. I try to avoid self-criticism and wishful thinking, too. You might call me conflict averse, which I understand is a popular contemporary term, but I'm not. I'm simply realistic.

And practical. That's my byword, my go-to behavior mode when all else fails. Bet may tease me about that habit, but I think she admires it, all the same.

Eve's finally asleep, worn out from emotional anguish. Bet's gone for a walk. I'm tidying the house, thinking about what I can pull together for supper. I'm also pondering.

Back in the day, we were taught to believe in one supreme being. We didn't question our form of faith.

Moses had delivered what seemed like a coherent message. One deity, instead of a bunch of local gods, goddesses and/or superstitions. It was easier than wondering which goddess was in charge of which specific boon. Besides, we felt secure and special. The word used was "chosen," which now seems horribly exclusionary. What happened to the people who weren't chosen? Were they kicked off the A team? Cast into utter darkness?

At the time, I didn't fret about the whys and wherefores of our belief system, or who was in and out. I simply went about my business, all of which you know.

Lately, though, I've begun wondering about the impetus toward faith. You may think that my lack of academic credentials makes me a dubious guide to a philosophical quandary. I don't see the query as academic, however. I see it as soul-driven.

I understand that many people nowadays have lost faith in the notion of an all-powerful being. There's been too much bloodshed, too much torture, too many children slaughtered: war upon war ever since Evie and Adam left their paradisiacal garden. Christians battling Muslims, Muslims waging war with Jews, nations throughout the globe conquering others, genocide, enslavement—and all somehow justified as being reasonable and right because a so-called deity declares it so. How can brutality be morally correct? How can it be ethical and ignored? Worshippers slaughtered in synagogues and mosques and churches ... shoppers shot down in malls ... concert goers and wedding guests dying within a hail of gunfire ...

I wish I could talk to some of those so-called Christians and persuade them to destroy those hideous guns. And then tell them that God-given rights shouldn't mean that first graders die in a barrage of bullets.

I wish all sorts of things—like being able share pictures of my grandkids on Facebook and Insta. But that's impossible. We didn't even have Brownie instamatics back then. Let alone cell phones.

It's reassuring seeing those happy images, isn't it? Birthday party celebrations, videos of babies' first words and tentative first steps, grandmas cuddling little ones. Makes you forget the world's ills.

Do men yearn for peace as much as women do? I have no idea.

Lot's Wife Returns

Shrouded as she must be ... but how would you envision her if death hadn't physically deformed her?

Well, not to human form because we all know what becomes of salted flesh. Consider the ancient mariners subsisting on salted beef and pork. Wouldn't they have preferred a handsome rib roast to that chewy bark-like substance? So ... Best not ask to see my face.

I'd like to consider Ruth's question. Forgive me if I skip about through eras and kingdoms. In the book of Exodus, there's a list of rules. They're all aimed at men. The first concerns seducing a virgin and being forced to pay the bride-price to her father. I'm using the written terminology, but let's be clear: isn't that supposed seduction exactly what Bathsheba endured? Could we please call it rape instead of using some dainty allusion?

Then there's a law for killing sorceresses (not sorcerers), and other regulations (quite a few in various sacred texts) about not mistreating aliens or oppressing them. Many of you political leaders failed that test, but then you were also instructed not to lie, deceive, or spread slander, pervert justice, or commit adultery. Sorry, the gong sounded and you all lost the bonus round.

I also consider enslaving people "oppressing" them, but I don't want to wade into those waters yet. I'll leave that up to the founding fathers of the United States of America.

But a through-line that most troubles me is the constant refrain about women as inferior creatures.

Poor Tamar, whom you recall from the book of Genesis, was mistaken as a shrine prostitute, which begs the question: If a guy heads off to worship at a holy site, shouldn't he be thinking about holy stuff, not cheating on his missus? Of course, Tamar's situation was especially dicey because the putz who bought the supposed sex worker's services was actually her father-in-law. I grant you that she was trying to turn the tables on him because her hubby had died and hoping to avoid the dismal fate of invisible, subservient widowhood, she needed to marry his brother. The old duffer promised to wed the two, then reneged, and Tamar chose her only course of action. Trick the guy. Have sex. Then blackmail him.

Naturally, that produced a big "woops" and "so, so sorry" from him. But that was *after* he'd declared that she should have been burned to death because she'd gotten preggers while she was a widow. In his book, that could only mean she was a prostitute. Huh? It was okay for him to screw her, but not for her to live!

Spoiler alert: Tamar survived. Her ruse worked. BUT, like I said, that's only because she had serious goods on her father-in-law. Call it blackmail if you want. I don't. I call it the truth.

By the way, she bore twins, which pleased the old goon endlessly. He liked to flap his lips about her righteousness and virtue. The height of hypocrisy in my mind.

I'm going to shut up now, because I'm fuming and would like to have a quiet moment.

~

So, let me introduce Queen Vashti. You know her as being revered by feminists and proto-feminists. As inspiring as her seminal act was, she was also a real person, not simply an icon. She needs to tell her story. Male historians and theologians have decried her as being narcissistic and immoral, just as they have me.

Vashti, my dear, you're up.

Vashti Talks

Vashti, the famous—or infamous according to your political stance. Enough said.

Thank you, Lottie. Cute nickname, don't you think? Sounds like Lotte Lenya. Didn't you love her as Pirate Jenny in *Three Penny Opera*? The sex worker who imagined getting her ultimate revenge. Fabulous piece of musical theatre. Fabulous mirror image of life.

A bit about me. Not the famous Queen Vashti, but me as a girl, then teen and finally young wife. I had the fortune—or misfortune—to be born of royal blood. Those of you who've followed the soap opera surrounding the current ruling family of Great Britain may empathize with the gilded-cage upbringing. Did I want to be set apart? Would you?

Jewels and costly garments are mini prisons. Even as a small child, I was expected to behave in a certain way. Imagine never, ever measuring up. That's how I felt. Small, nervous, always on edge.

All my caregivers were enslaved Jewish women. To say that they didn't like me would be an understatement. I forgot to mention that we lived in Babylon. My great-great grandfather was King Nebuchadnezzar II, who destroyed Jerusalem and the Jewish nation along with it. One of his chosen titles was King of the Universe. At the time, I didn't question that nomenclature. It was a matter of unassailable fact. Like living in a palace so vast I got lost in it. Or lessons in etiquette, poise, deportment and charm. How to turn the table at a dinner party, whom to seat where, etc. Or the total lack of parental love. They say that if you have never experienced something, you don't miss it. I'm not sure. I was lonely most of the time. I must have had an inkling that something was lacking.

I want you to understand I'm not asking for sympathy. I'm attempting to bring you into my world.

Then there's geopolitical warfare. None of which I understood then, but all of which shaped my existence. This isn't a lecture about Mesopotamia or Assyria or the importance of the Euphrates River as a trading hub. Since my time, there have been many other spots where one nation has battled another for control. I can name one: Iraq in what was once my homeland. Didn't Saddam Hussein plan to reconstruct the famed Ishtar Gate until the project succumbed to the American invasion?

In my mind's eye, I see two violent eras colliding: the Persians surrounding my home city and American troops dropping bombs on the presidential palace in

Baghdad, which led to amphibious assaults, civilian deaths, and death and dismemberment among all who fought. Those Marines, soldiers, pilots and crewmembers suffered greatly. Their leaders are to blame. Did none of them ask who the goddess Ishtar was, or what she represented?

If I seem to ramble, it's because I cannot separate the twin invasions. I hear screams and cries, smell burning flesh, feel the panic of not knowing where to flee. Or even how.

When I focus on my earliest memories, I watch the fabled Hanging Gardens of Babylon disappear in smoke, and the palace fill with enemy soldiers. "Run," I hear shouted from every room and corridor. "Run. Your father has been executed ..." Even as a girl, I understood blood lust. With no male to protect me, I've become an easy victim. Rape will be their kindest punishment. Rape and then slavery. For the first time in my life I experience the hopeless despair of my caregivers. I will become like them. Carted off. Abased. Misused. Tortured. If I misbehave.

~

I was lucky. I wonder whether Ishtar played a part. The goddess of both love and war. Because females are fierce when defending those in their care. Praying as I ran, I found myself face to face with the enemy's ruler, King Darius.

What was it in that unexpected encounter that saved me? My utter vulnerability? My tears? My terror? Or was it my choice garments and the jewels that marked me as royalty? On one side is kindness and sympathy. On the other, guile.

Lottie Takes Up the Tale

A setting is provided. Please alter if you wish.

But do not ignore this conversation.

"May I, Vashti? I know it's your story, but I also recognize how triggering this is for you." The voice is warm, encouraging, even bright but it emanates from an area of the room that's shrouded in darkness, rendering the speaker invisible—as is her preference.

Vashti nods, then sits, staring into a middle distance. It's clear from her posture that the setting is unfamiliar and discomfiting: an isolated, wooded, mountaintop cabin when she would have preferred a five-star resort in the Al Wadi Desert or the Hotel Ishtar on the Dead Sea. The chair, covered in brown Naugahyde, wobbles a bit on the uneven pine floorboards.

"A glass of wine, my friend? There's some chilling in the fridge."

"Later. Thank you. Maybe after we've Zoomed with Eve and the others." Smiling slightly, Vashti continues to gaze at nothing, her thoughts travelling inward and backward in time.

Unseen, Lottie also shifts in her seat. "Not quite what we bargained for, is it? This little retreat. Why do I feel as though we're in a witness protection program in the US of A? In an underfunded one at that. That fridge, for instance. A Sub-Zero would be preferable, by far."

"No amount of witness protection programs could have saved either one of us."

Lottie makes no answer.

Outside, a shutter rattles. A fir's bough brushes a window pane. A smell of dampness pervades the space. Vashti sighs.

"Are you familiar with the Russian author, Yevgenia Ginzburg, Vi?"

"Should I be?"

"Her works *Journey Into The Whirlwind* and *Within The Whirlwind* remind me of your story. Although she was a staunch communist, she opposed Stalin. A gigantic mistake. She was condemned to the Gulag."

"I would never have become a communist."

Lottie ignores the comment. "She served eighteen years there, but somehow managed to survive. One son died during the siege of Leningrad. He was fifteen. She never saw him after her arrest when he was eleven. She never even knew whether he believed her story or the lies spouted by Stalin's NKVD."

"The children always suffer the most, don't they?"

"How old were you when Darius captured you and decided to give you to his son?"

"Times were different back then."

"Were they?"

"Do you believe the cruelties that Ginzburg and other prisoners faced in Yaroslavl, or during the endless train trek east were different from inhumane acts from previous eras? Starvation, lack of water, box cars sidelined at every station so the local residents never learned the truth—"

"We didn't have box cars."

"Prison ships … forced marches while shackled in chains … They're no different. Yevgenia recited Pasternak's poetry to her box-car companions. She spoke until her voice gave out." Lottie pauses. "So … Darius awarded you to his son. Also a big muckety muck. But venal where Dad was … How would you describe him?"

"Authoritarian. Asexual, maybe? His focus was solely on conquering. He was good at that."

"And Sonsie?"

"Politically manipulative. I'd use the term womanizer, but what man wasn't in those days? Also a drunk."

"Sounds like a peach."

"What do you want from me?" Vashti spins toward her invisible companion. Her voice shakes with fury and sorrow. "True confessions? A salacious tale to pass the evening before we beam in with the other women? I'm tired of this nonsense. What happened, happened. I'm lucky I escaped."

"I'm not the enemy, Vi."

Vashti doesn't answer. A bitter groan fills the now darkening room. "Why is this damn place so badly lit? Stuck out in the middle of a goddamn forest, and the owners decided they didn't need a few extra lamps?

Lottie makes no reply. Vashti sighs again. "Sorry. I shouldn't lash out. You've had your share of grief."

"It's okay."

"No. It's not."

"Really, it is. You have every reason to be angry."

"He wanted me to parade around naked in front of all those courtiers and sycophants, all those supposed nobles and military brass. His queen, wearing a gussied-up crown and nothing else, walking through a sea of horny drunks. It makes me sick to think about what would have happened if I'd said yes."

"But you didn't."

"Not on your life! I told those creepy eunuchs he sent to fetch me to bugger off. Not that they could have—being eunuchs, and all."

"Weren't you worried about what might have happened next?"

"No. I was too outraged."

Lottie remains silent.

"I should have been. I still am. Dragged away from home when I was a girl, then dumped in this jerk's lap. He admired me for my beauty—that's what he said. A goddamn Miss Persia or Mesopotamia, or whatever." Vashti leaps up from her chair. "Gold and silver benches, gold goblets, mother-of-pearl, marble, porphyry, you name it: no expense spared. The guy absolutely loved to flaunt his wealth, his power over everyone. Me included! What kind of man summons the missus to prance around in her birthday suit? No need to answer that.

"I tried to make the best of it. I did. Before that, whenever he entertained his various groups of swells, I had the wives for dinner, or the weekend or the week. Made polite chitchat. Gave them the requisite gifts. Accommodated all their special diets, beauty regimes and all that crap. Tried to be a diplomat. Tried to act like a queen in charge of a kingdom. But I wasn't even in control of my own goddamn life ... I hope the jerk is rotting in Hell."

"Doubtful. Rich men get away with murder."

"Yes. And don't I know it." Vashti walks to a window and stares at the blackening panes. "That's the kicker, isn't it? Hubby confers with his wise guy attorneys and they decide to punish me because my actions might inspire other wives to rebel. Not kill me, which could turn me into a martyr, but send me packing, so that the other wives get the message and toe the line. Which they shouldn't have. They should have followed my example and said, 'No. No. No.' Instead, they stayed mum and I was banished. Then the wise guys went on the prowl to find another beautiful young virgin."

"Esther."

"Another dupe."

"Maybe not, Vi."

What Became of Esther?

Lottie and Vi wrestle with a complex question.

Join them.

"I'm not sure I agree that she an easy mark, Vi. Manipulated, certainly, but was she a wide-eyed innocent?"

Vashti doesn't immediately answer. "What other type of person would have fallen for my ex's stipulations. Lottie? She was forced to undergo endless beauty regimens to please the king. Doesn't that scream victimhood to you? Twelve months of being doused with ultra-pricey oil of myrrh as well as exotic perfumes and cosmetic treatments. Botox, boob implants. If the timing had been different—"

"*The Park Avenue Face.*"

"Naturally, she did as she was told. Total body make over, learning pointers on pleasing men from the other gals—"

"Concubines."

"A nice name for them. I would have used something less flattering. Finally, Esther appeared before the king who immediately started to pant and drool and then placed my crown on her head. I'm assuming she was dressed. I hope so."

"Her decision, though, wasn't it?"

"Was it, Lottie? That's what bothers me."

"She could have turned him down and walked away. Instead—"

"She was indoctrinated. Accept an elevated, wealthy status—albeit subjugation—or go home and become a burden on the penniless parents. Look at the women in India. Now as well as throughout history. Doweries, bride price ... put any name on the rotten practice that you wish. Those women don't opt to become victims, don't choose to be mere commodities, but they're forced to accept the reality that they have no autonomy. None. And the majority pay for their vulnerability with their lives."

"Esther didn't though."

"No. But don't forget she had a male secretly pulling strings for her. Her cousin, Mordecai. No one was aware of the situation—hubby included. Of course, I was long gone by then. Remember that Esther was a Jew. She kept her religion and background secret, then decided to use the king's fixation on her to save her people, which she did. 'Anything you want, my dear. Half my kingdom, dear girl.' Eventually, she had him hoodwinked."

"Which means she must have been extraordinarily clever, despite those absurd beauty treatments she agreed to undergo." Lottie pauses. "Or maybe Mordecai had been manipulating her from the beginning."

Vashti remains silent.

"Which would bolster your previous theory. Make her a double dupe, in fact."

"But ..." Vashti leans forward in her chair, her face creased in concentration. "What if she developed her own wiles and stratagems once she became queen? I did, after all."

"Possible. Was she as tough as you?"

"No idea. All I have is hearsay. My basic problem remains, though. Here's Vashti, the wife who once had Jewish captives as caregivers, and there's Esther, Miss Righteous Vindication, winning the day."

"Or Mordecai."

"Right."

Lottie laughs. "I shouldn't find this remotely amusing. And I don't. But your plight—and mine—seem inescapable. There you are, as you said, the former Queen Vashti, who represents the powerful, audacious female. Suffragists and authors of every genre and generation have recognized you—"

"But the guys still pull the strings."

Lottie doesn't answer. Instead, she starts humming "Pirate Jenny."

Listening, Vashti smiles. "I'm not critiquing her, L. In fact, I'm in awe of her cunning and strength of will.

Whoever she was when my ex plucked her out of the beauty pageant lineup, she survived both him and her cousin's machinations. But you see where this leaves me. Despised by my ex and every Jew who views Esther as a heroine. Yeah, I know, sounds kind of like an advice column gone haywire. *How come my ex's new in-laws, friends and colleagues hate me?* But it isn't that. I'd like to meet the woman. I'd like to become friends."

PART FOUR

The Sky Above the Ocean Is Blue

You will recognize the place and the players...

"Feeling better?" Ruth puts down her book as Eve steps out onto the porch. Bet places her pen atop the acrostic she's been filling in and looks at their hostess, her expression searching.

"I am, yes. Thanks. I didn't mean to go all drama queen on you."

Bet doesn't immediately speak. Instead, she continues to regard Eve. "You don't need to fake it with us, babe. The three of us have survived a lot of crap. No one here needs to pretend."

"I know that. I do."

"Do you? Truly?"

Eve faces her guest, her expression thoughtful. "I think so ..." The words are hesitant, the tone quiet.

"I'm not trying to insult you, so please don't take my words amiss. But I think that as the eldest you have a feeling that you need to protect us. Or placate or even manipulate us. But aren't we equals? By now, at any rate."

"I don't think Evie's condescending—"

"Not condescending, Ruthie. That wasn't my intention." Bet cocks her head. "I don't want to hurt anyone's feelings. But, well, I believe you're doing yourself a disservice by trying to be stoic. Especially around us."

"I wasn't being particularly stoic by bursting into tears."

"No. But you feel an apology is necessary. It's not. Really. And, if I'm brutally honest with myself as well as you, I don't like thinking that you've got more experience than we do. I'm not talking about your kids—"

"What, then?"

Bet moves toward the railing and looks out toward the beach. "Shall we take a stroll? It's a lovely day. Look how blue the sky is."

"What, then, Bet?"

"Shall we walk?"

Eve nods but presses the question as the trio starts down the stairs toward the path that leads to the beach.

"We come from entirely different backgrounds, don't we?" Bet brushes her hand across a feathered frond of dune grass as she walks, her expression more serious than even she realizes. "If we consider our places in history ... and the fact that we're generations upon generations apart. You, Eve, are the great-great-great grandmom. Then comes Ruthie, and finally me. But

I suggest that we're not stuck in those predetermined roles, just as we're not trapped in historical periods. Which means that you, Evie, wouldn't be older and wiser. Instead, you'd have experienced other events, in the same way that Ruthie and I grew up in different circumstances with distinct and diverse expectations."

Eve stops walking. "I'm following you."

"So, can't we consider ourselves equals in this cycle of life we find ourselves in?"

"But we are, Bet."

"Not really, honey. I don't believe you truly feel that way. You're still mom. I'm not trying to be mean. I'm only expressing my thoughts."

A seagull lofts overhead, calling to another. The three women gaze upward and follow the bird's flight.

"Do you think I'm overbearing, Bet?"

"Not that, no. But you don't need to behave maternally with us. We're your closest friends."

"And not my children."

"Not in the sense of being dependent upon you, no. Just like Vashti and Esther and Lot's maligned missus and every other woman throughout creation are both independent and interconnected."

Eve nods but doesn't speak. Ruth glances covertly at her, then away while Bet looks Eve full in the face.

"At this point in our lives, none of us need nurturing. We need a support system and love and respect among equals." She pauses. "Look. We enjoy these reunions, don't we? Well, here's something Ruthie suggested:

Why don't we include the others? I told her that we could reach them via Zoom or whatever this afternoon. Then next year, the three of us could join Vashti, Esther and Tamar and Lottie and Rachel and Leah and—"

Eve's lips form a rueful smile. "Which would preclude a pokey rental house and tuna melts … and antiquated jigsaw puzzles."

Bet continues to regard her friend as their path descends to the beach. "Those decisions would be the least of our considerations. We could find a resort that caters to women. Or a specialized retreat center. Think of what a blast we'd have gabbing and grousing with each other. Sure, things would be different, because you'd no longer be in charge, and we wouldn't be an exclusive threesome. But I, for one, think a larger group would be exhilarating. I'm also certain you've got their contact info."

Eve doesn't immediately answer.

Bet touches Eve's arm. "I'm not criticizing you, honey. I'm not. I understand who you are. And who you need to be. But I would dearly love to help you let yourself go. Be just one of us gals."

"Just one of the gals." She looks skyward. "How beautiful this is." Stretching her arms upward, she holds them aloft. "Just one of … Just one …" Then she spins in place and starts shedding her clothes. "A skinny dip, dear pals? What do you think?"

Ruth's jaw drops in consternation. "But the neighbors, Evie!" Her eyes widen with concern. In her mind, she hears Naomi's warnings regarding appropriate feminine behavior. Then those memories morph into something akin to rebellion. Although she continues to protest, her voice becomes an indecisive murmur. "But ..."

Eve chortles. "To hell with the neighbors."

By now Bet is also chucking off her clothes and laughing. "We're old women, hon. We've earned the right to do whatever we want!"

A Stage Four Cancer Survivor

Here an out-of-body experience may be necessary. Begrimed Manhattan subway tunnels filled with scurrying commuters as well as lush and colorful advertising posters.

A dichotomy of time and space.

The promotional posters in the subway concourse depict an idyllic beach getaway: glinting sands, young people and children cavorting in water that's a Disney ideal of aqua. One scene shows three women of differing nationalities who look to be middle aged (or older). With the ocean as a perfect backdrop, they smile at one another; and the skeptic in me wonders whether they were chosen as a nod to inclusivity and anti-ageism. They appear at peace with one another and the universe, but is that simply the ad agency's not-so-subliminal message that every woman should embrace her inner goddess? Throughout the long, insalubrious corridor, each model's face beams. Sunlight glows; clouds are puffy and cotton-white. A stark contrast from the sleety, gray winter day outside and the grim expressions of those rushing past me. New York is not known for camaraderie among strangers.

I should know. I introduced myself before. Moira: middle grade teacher and so forth. I didn't mention that I lived in Greenwich Village for a short time, prior to my graduate school days and career.

Hurrying along, I glance at the advertisements, feel a palpable longing for balmy climes, and then push ahead. I've just come from the funeral of a friend who died far too young, and need to catch a commuter train and return home. It's been a long, sad day.

A subway has just pulled in as I rush down the steps. "Is this the E?" I ask as I straddle the entrance.

A seated woman nods and smiles. I jump aboard. She moves aside to give me space to sit, and there begins a friendship that is to last two years until her death.

~

Essie was her name, short for Esther, which she found too old-fashioned, but which had belonged to an elderly relative her parents had revered. As a Korean-American, she understood that generational reverence was mandatory. Essie was a successful businesswoman, married with three teenage kids. And a survivor of stage four cancer—uterine papillary serous carcinoma—as she subsequently explained in an email.

But I'm getting ahead of myself and that fateful encounter.

Our journey lasted for—what—maybe thirteen minutes at most, during which we talked nonstop. Essie had just come from Sloan Kettering. She had good news: still in remission! She was upbeat and eager to share her optimism and her hopes for the future. She'd been diagnosed five years prior, had a background in research science and statistics, and was in the midst of writing about her newly found sense of positivity and empowerment. She wanted to help other women and their families.

Her story and energy enfolded me. I felt that this chance meeting had been pre-ordained. As I explained earlier, as an Irish-American, the spirit world is very real to me. The thin spaces, where the separation between earth and the mystical and holy, are easy to cross.

In my mind, she and I had been destined to meet. I could have jumped aboard any other car on the subway, or missed the E train altogether. She might not have glanced up from the book she'd been reading. I would have returned home in silence, and she would have, as well.

Pulling into Penn Station, we exchanged hurried phone/email info. I promised to aid her in any way I could. She promised to send me her draft manuscript. Then we parted and ran to catch our homeward-bound trains.

~

Essie and I were in almost weekly contact for a year. I sought out publishing friends for advice, but no one seemed to want a story about cancer—even a positive one. That didn't keep me from trying to buck the system. I read her work, sent many *Brava!* messages.

At length her symptoms returned and our communications grew sporadic. She understood that she was dying. I tried to email empathetic thoughts, but the efforts felt contrived.

And then she was dead.

I have her manuscript still. I cherish it. I cherish that strange and wondrous moment of connection, and I ponder how two total strangers managed to intersect and interact.

Did we know each other during previous lives? Were we friends in some distant and forgotten past? Or relatives? I believe so. I wish I could go back in time and untangle the threads of our dual existences.

Here's to you, Esther, wherever your soul abides. I trust we shall meet again. And I firmly believe we will recognize a shared connection.

Eve Interrupts Moira's Story

Please give Eve space and a place in which to recall and recount.

She may not need an established physical surrounding.

Eve has transcended time.

A bit more information on Moira: After a somewhat rocky childhood, she was fortunate to be able to create the life she wanted. The kid thing has consumed her as it did me. I make no mention of her mate, not because he's bad or absent or cruel, but because, by necessity, her focus doesn't include him. He's a bit like Adam. Well-meaning but not particularly useful in a situation that demands action, initiative, and drive.

You see, one of her kids was born with a birth defect and suffered grand mal seizures starting at three months old. Her life spun, dropped, and swiveled. Fun mom, pop, kiddie, ice-cream-and-cake days vanished. Healing became central and remains central.

She doesn't talk about it, so I will. We mothers need to care for one another.

The birth defect required surgery. Back in my day, no such thing, but for Moira an obvious solution. Painful, scary, but self-evident. The seizures were another thing.

After the first seizure, the docs put the baby on meds. Phenobarbital, I believe. Again, I'm a newbie with this type of information.

Moira hated what the meds did to her child. The active infant became a sleeping, unresponsive lump. No reaching for objects, no smiles or recognition of other stimuli. She expressed her concerns during regular EEGs but was ignored. This situation continued for two months: mom fretting, docs mouthing platitudes. At the end of that time, she was told that her baby had probably suffered severe brain damage during an early seizure and would never "experience normal activity."

She determined that prediction would never come true.

But what to do?

She's a smart, educated woman, but not a physician. Medicine was like—um, maybe an aspirin to help ease a headache or menstrual cramps? Or a baby aspirin for a teething child? So, now, this awful stuff that leaves her child in a vegetative state? No! No way in hell!

She did what I would have done under the circumstances. She chucked the meds. And didn't tell the docs.

Instead, she watched for signs that her baby might begin to seize. She became proficient at the task, which is why her mate became secondary. Her other kids, too. That neglect caused and still causes her grief, which makes her overcompensate, but she was and is determined to give her baby a normal life.

A flicker of the eye, a tremble of one hand, a sense that her baby was losing focus: Moira was all over the situation. She'd murmur the little one's name, stroke arms, legs, cuddle—anything to bring her child back into what she considered "the conscious world."

Sometimes, she'd stretch one hand skyward, while enwrapping her child with the other. "God's going to heal you," she'd whisper. "I can feel God's presence. It's like electricity. And I'm holding you within it."

In fact, I was the one she was reaching toward.

is why her mate became so [illegible]. Her [illegible] kids, [illegible] [illegible] and still [illegible], which makes her [illegible] but she [illegible] determined to give her baby [illegible] life.

A [illegible] the band [illegible] was [illegible] at [illegible] [illegible] could [illegible] what she [illegible]

[illegible]

[illegible]

[illegible] was reaching toward [illegible]

Deborah Demands to Be Heard

As the women continue to gather ...

Ah, yes, motherhood. Lovely. Demanding. Fulfilling. Heartening, as well as frightening. A lifetime role.

That wasn't my job. By choice, I'm a warrior. Deborah is my name. Picture me in any military garb you wish: tailored uniform adorned with campaign medals, bronze breastplate, plumed helmet, armed Amazon regalia. Travel though time. Not as many of us female generals, admirals, commanders out there as there should be, are there? But we have existed and still do. We're braver than hell. We have to be. We're fighting "this man's army," as well as an enemy.

I'm also a prophet, judge and visionary. The sole female judge in the early Hebrew texts, which is a momentous achievement. My name translates to "bee," which you may equate to the pugilist Muhammad Ali's famous line: "Float like a butterfly, sting like a bee." That's me.

The famed "Song of Deborah" is full of fire and a battle of which I'm rightfully proud.

In short, I was and remain no one to mess with.

Let me supply some historical background. A king of Canaan subjugated the Israelites—my people—abasing them, filling them with fear, and knocking the stuffing out of them in every respect (including their self-respect).

Naturally, I was outraged. I summoned a general named Barak (not Obama) and told him to gather ten thousand troops and defeat the forces of Sisera, the commander of the SOB's army.

Barak demurred, said he wouldn't fight without me joining in the battle. Why did he dither? I'll leave you to answer that question. As top brass, I outlined my stipulations: I'm in charge, so any resultant victory would belong to me, a woman. Agree? Yes: I'm good to go. No: You're on your own.

He consented to my conditions without a second thought. Read into his acquiescence what you want.

Troops readied. Battle fought. Sisera's army whomped. S. hightailed it while his soldiers continued to struggle along and then finally fled. (Cut to Napoleon pulling the same stunt in Russia, scarpering while his *grande armée* starved and froze and dropped in their tracks.)

Eventually, that coward S. found himself near the tent of Jael, another kick-ass female warrior. He whimpered that he needed some water. She gave him milk (in a handsome goblet, no less) whereupon he fell asleep. Dumb schmuck.

Jael then grabbed a tent pin and pounded it through the guy's temple. Not an easy task: bone being bone and all, and timing being critical. If he'd woken up … But he didn't. Skull split apart. End of Sisera.

End of Canaan's dominance.

Here's part of the conclusion of my song—after the bit about Jael offing Gen'l S. Sorry it's not in Hebrew, but this English version came to hand. As you can imagine, I'm not a bookish type.

> "The mother of Sisera cried through the lattice,
> Why is his chariot so long in coming?
> Why tarry the wheels of his chariots?
> Her wise ladies answered her,
> Have they not divided the spoil?
> A damsel, two damsels for each man …"

Disgusting, right? But accepted protocol. Damsel is a deceptively frilly word, but the reality remains. Women as spoils for the guys on the winning team.

~

Ah, here's Jael to corroborate her story. Take a good look at her. If you're expecting a resemblance to the Wonder Woman franchise, think again. Jael is real, flinty, fierce, and despite that stellar job she did on Sisera, never cruel. Most women aren't. No thumping of chests. No metallic balls hung from the backs of our pick-up trucks, no cut-off body parts, dried and kept as souvenirs.

Jay doesn't go in for posturing or pretense. She doesn't need to.

But let us continue.

Delilah—our estimable friend—take it away. Jay and I applaud you.

Samson and Delilah: Fact vs Fiction

Who would be the perfect casting for this role?

To borrow from the Gershwins' showstopping tune "Sam and Delilah" in their musical *Girl Crazy*, Delilah—that would be me—was a "floozy." The aforementioned Sam was cast as a rowdy broncobuster type. Ethel Merman, then an unknown performer, brought down the house while belting out that ditty, which was aptly titled—as above.

The thing is I wasn't a floozy or hooker or sex worker. Not then. Not now. Not ever. I wonder what Ethel (no callow Minnie Mouse herself) thought of the lyrics. I'm assuming she must have been cheering me on. "Good on ya, sweetie. Get that sucker and show him what's what."

Which I did. As we all know.

Given that Deb and Jael just finished offing Commandant Sisera, it's my cue to describe how I softened up Strongman Samson.

One big question before I start, though. The 1949 flick starring Hedy Lamarr as me and Victor Mature as himself strikes me as curious in its timing. I'm not saying I didn't enjoy the film. Hedy's gorgeous. Maybe not *precisely* my type, but I'm not complaining. In fact, I'm happy that a movie star wanted to do my biopic. But why 1949?

WWII emboldened us gals. We found meaningful vocations for which we were lauded: Rosie the Riveter, for one, as well as countless British, French, Polish, Sufi and German special ops and double agents. So why make a costume drama/bodice ripper about a supposed strumpet?

I get it that the world needed a hit of amnesia after all that carnage and A bombs and what not, but was a floozy necessary? And a foreign one, at that. Am I missing a hidden message here? Don't bring your war bride home to Mama's lace-doilied house? Or: Ladies, get back into the kitchen where you belong? Which is precisely what happened during the subsequent decade.

Feel free to ponder away while I rev up the time machine.

So, Samson … Not exactly a lovable hunk. Built, I grant you. But, really, would you fall for a gym bunny merely because he had ginormous pecs, or would you prefer a little conversation mingled in with the perfect abs?

Mr. Universe didn't believe in small talk. He liked us females, but mostly just for the sex part, which is why

I get this rap about being a hooker. And another thing that makes me bitter is that some hoity-toity, celibate, early Christian saint said that I represented the evil that befalls men who marry out of their faith. He (and my other detractors) insisted that I was a Philistine, which has never been proven. Sam, on the other hand, was to the manner born—being Hebrew, and all.

He had a mean streak, though, and liked to play cruel jokes on folks, even his first wife—and that was right after the nuptials. I heard she cried for days. In fact, her father decided to rescue the poor kid and give her to another guy, which made Samson so jealous he lashed out at everyone: Dad, ex-wife, animals, and all the family's worldly goods.

This is how the plot went down: Sam captured three hundred foxes, tied them up two by two and tail to tail, affixed burning torches to them and let them loose to burn acres of grain and olive groves and vineyards. It's unnecessary to tell you what became of the poor beasts.

A small aside: I love reading 19th and 20th century novels, but when I get to a character that's cruel to animals I recoil and thereafter despise that person. If the foxes' scheme upset you, it did me, too.

Oh, and another aside: Dad and ex-spouse were subsequently burned to death by the Philistines.

Now we come to me.

As you know, Samson was famous for being ripped and brawny. He escaped all sorts of dangerous scrapes simply by using physical strength. His enemies couldn't figure out the source of that power. No anabolic steroids back then. No erythropoietin, no hGH or GHB. It was my job to get the skinny on the big guy's brawn. I used sex, natch, but he was cagey and lied. I whined, cajoled, nagged until I learned the truth: It was the man bun!

I cut it off while the dude was sleeping. And voila! As weak as a kitten. Weaker, in fact.

I do regret that the Philistines decided to gouge out his eyes when they captured him. Unnecessary cruelty to my thinking. But I viewed my role as an undercover agent, NOT a military honcho. I'll make no comment on their decision to allow his hair to grow back. But they did.

The rest you know. Or you know according to whatever religion penned my story. I was a serial floozy. Or a heroine.

Your choice. I know where the truth lies.

PART FIVE

Don't Look Away

Pushed to the Limit

Where is God? I hear you whimper. *We pray, but our words are in vain … or our faith is too weak.* You blame your fickleness when moments of salvation fail to occur and subsequently blame me and then lose hope that a deity exists who will comfort and rescue you.

Listen to me.

I cannot rescue you from your current lunacies. You rely on fossil fuels, incinerate everything you can, drop bombs on one another thereby further polluting the planet. To say nothing of your worship of plastic! The Adoration of the Magi reimagined as representatives from Big Business hovering over a baby's crib that's overflowing with bottles and spray cans of herbicides, pesticides, antifreeze, microwaveable takeout food containers, asbestos, etc., etc. Of course, there's no room for an infant in that scene. The infant is dead.

Your politicians lie, your corporations wallow in deceit. You still venerate the glass ceiling. Haven't you been paying attention to the women telling this tale? Is their message failing to pierce your thick skulls, or are you purposely ignoring it?

I told you before that I was exasperated by your dissembling, your hoaxes, your barbarity, your ravening greed. You create and sell videos of people torturing baby monkeys; you laud influencers who promote chauvinism, sex trafficking and violence. Read the headlines in your newspapers. Watch gossipy tell-alls and scandal mongering on your devices. Then tell me if I'm wrong to say all that is contemptible has coalesced within your bodies and brains.

Perhaps Noah should return, and your home again sink under the seas.

But DON'T call it "global warming."

Eve Intuits Disaster

"God's in trouble," are the first words Eve utters as she begins stepping out of the ocean. The receding and breaking waves pool around her knees and then ankles, stirring up sand that momentarily clouds the clear water. She looks down at her wet body as if uncertain where she is.

"What do you mean?" Bet cocks her head. Her dark glasses conceal her eyes, but it's clear she finds the message humorous and a bit absurd. "TLGA can't be in trouble, sweetie. Trust me. David might have gotten in Dutch for crossing the Holy Mightiness, but the relationship wasn't remotely equal. Ditto for that guy Job. And Absalom—"

Eve grabs a beach towel. "We need to do something."

"Besides, if you'd let me finish what I was going to say, you told us you don't believe in TLGA any longer. Or pray. Or words to that effect."

Eve's expression turns dour as she rubs herself down. "Not the same thing. Something's going on. And it's not good."

Bet sighs. "Oh, Evie. A skinny dip. A nice, mellow afternoon. Don't get all in a kerfuffle about some imagined—"

"I'm not asking you to understand. I'm not sure I do, either. I just want you to listen—"

"Trying to, hon, but your lead-in stumped me. Kind of like saying, 'The global military-industrial complex is in trouble.'"

"It would help if you'd be serious once in a blue moon."

"Touché. But I'd also like to enjoy our communal vacay instead of stewing about a supposed being—or thing—that never gave a rat's fuck about me. Or maybe all of us 'ladies.'"

Ruth looks from one friend to another. She fingers the towels she'd folded across her chest and the other wrapping her shoulders, then pulls the edges tighter and shivers as the sun dodges behind a cloud. "If Evie's concerned, maybe ..."

"How about we enjoy post-dip mimosas, instead of fretting about—"

"I'm serious, Bet."

"I see that."

"And I also appreciate your desire for equality among us women."

"Good."

"This is different, though. This isn't about us."

Bet doesn't reply.

"I'm not pulling rank. Or trying to mother you. Or suggesting I'm smarter. I'm simply stating a fact."

Bet draws in a breath. "Which is that God—a thing—is in trouble. Like this beach is in trouble—"

"Due to climate change, certainly—"

"C'mon, babe. It's a gorgeous day. Let's not waste it fretting about hypotheses."

Eve turns away from the others and begins walking toward the rental house.

Ruth starts to follow her. Bathsheba remains behind.

"Ruthie, while you're at it, grab the bubbly and OJ from the fridge. The glasses are chilling, too. And, Evie, please get this nonsense out of your brain. You're too wise a woman to get in a lather about gods and goddesses or demons and sprites or any of those contrivances."

~

Eve doesn't speak as she hurries up the walkway and climbs the steps. Ruth lags behind, then crosses the porch toward the stairs leading down to the rear yard and the drying line. Drawing abreast of her friend, she reaches for her soggy towel, but Eve shakes her head, her face taut with worry.

Enwrapped in dampness and anxiety, she stands, staring back toward the ocean. Her body quivers with something other than cold.

"But how do you know about this supposed trouble, Evie?"

"I heard a voice crying out while I was swimming."

"Oh ..." Ruth follows her friend's gaze. The water is devoid of human activity: no sailboat or paddleboarder, no snorkeler or swimmer or angler casting a line from the shore. "Like a voice from history? I mean, didn't you say that this part of the beach once had shipwrecks?"

"No. It was present. Real. Now."

"But … God? I mean. Look, I don't want to sound skeptical, but—"

"I've heard God speaking before. You know all about that. This sounded the same."

"Yes, but that was a very long time ago, ages and ages, in fact. And—"

"And the world was different back then?"

"It was. Entirely."

"Was it? Aren't women still suffering the same kinds of abuse that you and Bet and the others did?"

"Of course, they are. That's a fact of life."

"Why, though?" Eve's lips tighten. She doesn't expect an answer but needs to speak her peace.

"Let's put that dilemma on hold for a moment, Ru." She shakes her head; her expression remains tense. "Remember when you told me about how close you and Naomi were. You could intuit each other's thoughts—both of you waking up in the middle of the night fretting over some problem you believed the other was enduring?"

Ruth nods. Eve glances away. Her shoulders slump.

"Maybe, I'm wrong. As you said, my encounter with God was a long time ago. Perhaps some fundamental elements have remained, like misogyny and oppression and so forth. But perhaps, others such as species interconnectedness and reliance on intuition have become outmoded or even suspect."

Ruth reaches up a hand and massages her friend's shoulder. "You need to stop fretting, sweetie. You can't save the world."

"I couldn't even save my sons."

Ruth doesn't speak. Glancing across the garden, she also shivers. The once-sunny day is turning grayer by the minute.

"You did the best you could. We all do the best we can."

"Do we? Or do we merely stumble along? Win some? Lose some and hope no one is keeping score?"

"Don't each of us keep a personal score? Don't we mark down our successes and failures and our times of cowardice and inconstant hopes? I know I do."

"I'm not sure I agree. Is Bet given to moody self-reflection? I concur with her assessment of me as being overly controlling, but then the next minute she turns flippant as if she's embarrassed of having deeper thoughts."

"Don't be hard on her, Evie. She likes the façade she created. Needs it, in fact." Pausing, she looks her friend full in the face. "God's an idea, honey, a theory, if you will, not a physical being. Of course, I understand the religious stuff: miracles and all that. But that's only because people like believing that something big and powerful has their back. As much as you want to draw parallels between Naomi and me as mutually supportive relatives, God—whatever that concept is—isn't and wasn't your parent or in-law or relative of any kind."

She pauses again.

"Don't take this amiss, but I wonder whether that voice you originally heard, the one yelling at Cain, was a figment of your imagination. You'd just experienced an enormous tragedy; doesn't it make sense that you weren't thinking clearly? Or even hallucinating?" She tilts her head, judging her friend's reaction. Her expression is soothing and soft. "Besides, where are you going to begin on this rescue mission of yours? Stairway to heaven?"

"I'm being serious, Ruth."

"I understand that, but, as I said—and Bet, too—maybe it's time to lighten up."

Eve remains silent, her expression still pensive.

"You're not responsible for every person who walks the face of the earth."

"I know that."

"Sometimes, though, it seems as if you feel that you are ... centuries and centuries of us. I'll repeat Bet's advice. We're not your kids. We're our own people. Making our own mistakes." Stretching out her hand, she feels raindrops. "Let's go inside. It looks like it's about to pour. I'll grab an umbrella and fetch Bet before that fancy caftan of hers gets ruined."

Distant lightning ricochets off the ocean as Ruth opens the door. "Uh oh, it appears the weather may put the kibosh on our Zoom call."

Watch Out

"Oh, for pity's sake!" Coming out of nighttime darkness, Bet's bitten words are the epitome of personal pique. "Now we've lost power. Looks like the entire neighborhood has. And, for some obscure reason, my cellphone's on the fritz." Her bedroom door bangs shut behind her. Unseen, she draws in a rapid, irate breath. "What is this, hell house?"

"My cell died, too." Ruth is also invisible. "Evie? Are there candles or hurricane lamps or something in this joint?"

A bang followed by an oath reveals that their hostess is on the first floor. "Damn, I forgot about that table." The sound of a drawer being pulled out ends in another crash. "Ouch! Lucky the entire sideboard didn't topple over. I found the candles, though ... and matches."

A flickering light moves to the bottom of the staircase. Eve's face is illuminated. In a nightgown but no wrapper, she looks perturbed as she glances upward toward her guests. "Can you two make it down here? Or do you need your own candles?"

A searing jolt of lightning tears across the garden. The house shakes. "Sounds like the storm's right on top of us." Ruth holds onto the banister as she gingerly descends the wide, uncarpeted staircase. "I don't recall anything in the forecast that called for this kind of weather."

Bet laughs as she also descends. "I guess Evie was right. Someone whose-name-shall-not-be-mentioned is royally pissed."

Eve remains silent.

Bet adds an apologetic. "I'm royally pissed, too. No cell service. No electricity. Back in the Dark Ages, I guess."

Rain sheers sideways into the windows, battering the shutters. The wind's roar increases, becoming all but deafening. Eve shields her candle with cupped fingers. "Maybe we should move into the kitchen and away from all this glass."

As they do, they hear something large and heavy, either a tree or sizeable limb, fall onto their parked car, crushing it. The noise of metal twisting into metal momentarily outpaces the wind.

"The rental company's not gonna like that. We can claim act of God, but it's our word against a tree." Bet tries for a chuckle as she wraps her silk dressing gown tighter. Finished with the garment, she tosses her long hair out of her face and affixes a self-possessed, if forced, smile. "You two ever sing this one: 'The Lord said to Noah, there's gonna be a floody, floody ...'"

Ruth draws in a nervous breath. "Maybe we should hang out in the cellar and wait for this thing to pass."

"Or we can get raptured up if we linger near the windows." Then Bet turns serious. "Are violent storms common around here, Evie?"

~

There'd been no need for the women to set foot in the home's basement before, and they find it larger than they'd imagined. The space is also surprisingly clean although crowded with furniture no longer in use, as well as bikes without wheels, battered paddleboards and broken oars, snorkeling gear with clouded masks, fishing rods minus reels, furled sails and a six-foot high pile of suitcases affixed with antiquated hotel and ocean liner labels.

Bet touches an oar with one manicured finger. "Those valises are fun, but why would anyone save a piece of crap like this? It looks like a shark bit it in half."

Their three candles flicker in the darkness while they grope their way, hoping to find serviceable chairs piled amongst the furnishings.

"No way I'm perching in this dingy hole." Bet puts down her candlestick. Then she returns to her song. "'So, Noah, he built him, he built him an arky, arky …'"

Eve sighs, the sound pointed.

"Just trying to lighten the mood, hon. I thought the flood reference was clever."

Ruth's perky voice breaks an incipient stalemate. "Hurricane lamps. Let's hope there's still oil in them."

The lamps are lit, but the room becomes stranger as the corners reveal more castaway possessions.

Bet frowns. "How old is this damn place, anyway?"

A gust of wind shakes the cellar's storm doors. Then tree limbs crash downward, their branches scraping the building's shingled walls while the limbs themselves thud against the sloping doors.

"I guess Eve's correct. The powers that be are having a hissy fit." Bet tries for a laugh but fails. "Not sure I would have visited if I knew we were in for a hurricane, or nor-easter, or medicane or whatever you call them in this neck of the woods. When we decide to gather all of us gals together, let's find a resort that's sheltered. And no tents like Jael's, either. Glamping may be a 'thing,' but it's not for me."

"There were no predicted weather events that I heard." Ruth monitors the storm doors as she speaks. "I think we should stay as far away from them as we can. If they shatter, we're liable to get badly hurt."

"This is going to play havoc with our nude ocean frolics." Bet attempts another laugh.

Eve makes no response. Turning her back on her guests, she begins exploring the space.

Above them, the house continues to bear the brunt of the storm.

"TLGA wouldn't be personally enraged at you, would he, honey?"

Eve stops her exploration and looks Bet full in the face. "Why do you refer to God as a he?"

Despite the leaden stare, Bet laughs in earnest. "Don't tell me you've succumbed to this LGBTQIA—"

"I'm serious. Why do you use a male pronoun for—"

"Because everyone does, hon. De rigueur and all that—"

"Not in my book. And, for your information, LGBTQIA is a crucial step in self-determination. Everyone has a right to be their own person. And make their own—"

"C'mon, Evie. I don't want to fight. Besides, I should be the last person to challenge individual rights, don't you think? I'm only trying to inject a bit of humor into what feels like a dangerous situation. Worshipping idols was a 'thing,' once, too, and—"

"And women's suffrage."

"Honey, let's not argue. I traveled a long, looong way and spent a lot of dough—"

"I repeat: a 'thing' like women's suffrage, or wildlife trafficking, or global warming, or—"

"Speaking of which—"

"I'm not joking, Bet."

"Have it your way, then. TLGA's a gal just like us. Big boobs, sequined gowns, a tiara—"

"I understand that you've had to cope with heinous experiences. Uriah, David, all that ugliness. And I recognize you have every right to be cynical, but just for once, can't we—"

"Right. Ditch the tiara."

"Can't we have a serious conversation?" Eve's words disappear as another boom rips through the cellar, immediately followed by the acrid scent of stale wood smoke, pouring down the flue that connects to the fireplace and oil heater.

Ruth gasps. "The chimney must have fallen."

"Lucky we weren't roasting marshmallows." Despite the effort at a jest, Bet's lips quiver.

Eve's eyes pinch in irritation. "I'm going back upstairs." She turns toward the steps. Neither of her friends follow.

Where Are You?

Stumbling upstairs to the first floor and then cautiously ascending to the second, Eve recognizes how perilous this choice is. She takes some solace in the fact that the home wasn't built closer to the sea and the ever-expanding scope of the tidal surge, but the age of the structure worries her. Windows could blow out, or trees fall onto the roof. She wonders whether the old rafters are firm or whether they're insect riddled and decides the latter is likely.

From the second floor, she climbs up a rickety flight of stairs into the attic, probably the worst place of all to ride out a hurricane, but one she needs to return to. Prior to Ruth and Bet's arrival, she visited the space on a whim and found an antique baby's crib and a trunk filled with a boy's clothes that ranged from infancy to eight or nine years old. All were outmoded and indelibly creased by years of storage. The discovery rattled her; she vowed to let the building's secrets remain intact.

Now, she feels compelled to spend time with this vanished child. She understands that she's being irrational but fears that the tempest will frighten him. His ghost, that is. It was clear to her that the child had died, and that grief had consigned the remnants of his short life to a forgotten storage space.

For reasons she can't comprehend, her memory cycles back to a baby bird she encountered long ago in another lifetime and another space. A house sparrow, the smallest of three. The mother couldn't cope with the demands of the larger two who kept pushing their sibling away as she attempted to feed all three. The result had been predictable but terrible to witness. The little thing had hopped about, tried a few short flights, picked up stray seeds, but didn't know how to crack and eat them. Watching, Eve's eyes had welled with tears. The baby bird heard her and fluttered close. Its eyes were rheumy, its feathers tattered; desperation shook its tiny body. Images of abandoned children, failure-to-thrive kids and abused kids filled her mind. "Little one," she whispered.

"Little one," she now murmurs. Then, "Abel? Cain? Boys, where are you?"

If the wind screams and tears at the roof tiles, she doesn't hear it. She's lost to everything but her living sorrow.

~

And where is God while Eve relives this anguish? In the attic. In the wind. In the trees that sway and break. In the ocean thrashing the shoreline, the boulders weighting the beaches, the pebbles flung by pounding waves, in each seabird hunkering down, each crow trying to hide. God circles above and within, wailing, weeping, screaming in wrath and despair.

"Oh, my beloveds. Oh, my beloveds. What have you done? What have I done?"

The Glass House

In silence, Eve, Bet and Ruth step onto the now-battered porch. They don't speak as they peruse the destruction of the prior day and night. The structure is still sound, but every table, chair, settee, and recliner has been either splintered or whisked away by the wind. What remains is a jumble of unusable furniture.

The sky, however, is an exquisite cobalt blue, the sun brilliant; everything glimmers: the crushed car, the lawn now strewn with leaves, branches and vines of infinite variety, as well as the mud clinging to the roots of overturned trees. The wind has settled into an apologetic breeze. Tomorrow it will carry the scent of corruption, but not today. Whatever living thing, whether animal or plant, that perished during the storm is awaiting consecration.

As the three women stand amidst the storm's detritus, residents in neighboring houses also emerge. All also remain silent. No one attempts to rectify the damage: clear water from storm drains, retrieve broken porch furniture, assess roofless garages, verandas torn asunder, ruined flower beds, and flattened streetlamps.

That will come, but not yet.

For now, speech is inconsequential.

Her jaw set, Eve sets a course to the beach. Bet and Ruth follow, albeit unwillingly. No one questions her decision. They simply walk behind her, single file and slowly. Streams that yesterday meandered through the marshes leading toward the dune have become engorged into small rivers. All carry leafed branches that race toward the sea. Wading is perilous. Broken chairs, punctured soccer balls, cracked window frames, a drowned teddy bear eddy in plummeting zigzags, catch in the mud and hurtle forward.

Eve is determined. Her friends trail in her wake, Bet the more timorous. She's dressed in a summery skirt, but the top is ill-matched and rumpled as if she grabbed whatever clothes came to hand.

Crossing the beach is difficult. Full-grown tree trunks have been thrust upon it as though they were the slimmest of twigs. The waves are mountainous. When they break upon the changed landscape of sand and rock, the earth shakes. Salt spray stings the eyes; flung upward, the fine mist also dazzles. No sea birds have yet taken to the skies. Without their calls, the scene has a funereal quiescence.

Eve walks as far out toward the water's edge as she dares. There's no wading even knee-deep today. She knows the undertow will be fierce. Bet and Ruth eventually reach her. They join hands, then stand closer, tightly wrapping their arms across one another's shoulders and inclining their heads toward one another's. No one says a word. Instead, they gaze seaward and then toward a cliff upon which perches a glass-fronted, architecturally perfect home, the coveted jewel of the area.

The lawn and garden fronting it have vanished into a rocky beach below. The angle of repose protecting the property has become a gash of raw earth and tumbling boulders; and the pergola that hosted formal evening receptions and lavish luncheons has slid halfway down through the brown muck: a jumble of cedar beams and teak settees that look as haphazard as dropped matchsticks. The house's vaunted deck now dangles unsupported. Below it, only sky.

As the women watch, the house begins tilting seaward. The movement is slow, nearly unidentifiable. Residents flee from the main, landside entry. Too far away to hear, they look small and frenzied. Some raise their hands to the sky; others continue dodging backwards; all stare at the home as its inexorable descent begins.

Sliding into the abyss, the house rips out its foundation. Down the glass walls crash; down veer the floors and roof. All collapse in a headlong race along a growing black-brown gash that yesterday held pine trees and sculpted walkways and shaded lookout points.

The beach, flat and finite, ends the flight, and the waves, like giant fingers, claw the remnants of the doomed house into the depths.

The three women don't move, don't make a sound. Their arms, still encircling one another, are frozen in place.

"Be still," Eve hears as plainly as though it were Bet or Ruthie talking to her. She doesn't turn to look at them. The voice belongs to neither.

"Be still and know that I am God."

Gazing at the ocean, Eve utters a soundless, *Yes.*

Reader's Guide

The Bible referenced is the American Standard Version (ASV).

The Saint Helena Psalter employs inclusive, expansive language. God is never referred to with a masculine pronoun. Reading that translation is revelatory.

Questions:

Eve:

How does her story evolve?

In what ways does grief figure in Eve's core being?

In the chapter, "Eve Alone," she says, "We wives, concubines, mistresses make do, don't we? We carry on. Make the beds, sweep the house. But often we do so at the risk of avoidance. It's easier to cook dinner than to search out core problems and work to heal them. Easier to pin our faith on hope no matter how tremulous." Do her words resonate with you? And/or disturb you?

Do you see modern correlations?

What about Adam's relationship to his sons?

If you consider Eve as part of an ancient tribal culture, how might her societal situation affect her decisions?

As a contemporary woman, could she have intervened and prevented Cain's crime?

Ruth:

Ruth understands that she's an alien. What are her options for survival? Have they changed over the centuries? If not, why?

In the chapter, "Ruthie Speaks Up," she admits she's the most conventional of the three women. She also declares she's realistic and tries to find hope and avoid self-criticism and wishful thinking. Eve and Bathsheba believe those traits make Ruth overly optimistic. What do those labels evoke regarding self-image versus group image?

Bathsheba:

Consider that Bathsheba was a victim who bore the blame. What parallels do you see with her story and contemporaneous events such as the #MeToo movement?

What about other persistent gender constraints?

In the chapter, "Eve Intuits Disaster," Ruth tells Eve, "You did the best you could. We all do the best we can."

Eve replies: "Do we? Or do we merely stumble along? Win some? Lose some and hope no one is keeping score?"

What do these conversations say about individual judgments and interpretations of others' actions? Or about divided loyalties?

How do Ruth and Bet interpret one another's motives/choices?

Eve observes that Bet likes and needs the façade she created.

Are there additional facades within the tale? Does God have one?

Describe a time when you used or needed a façade. What did you gain or lose from that experience?

God:

How does it feel to envision a nonbinary God? Freeing or challenging? Why?

Has God attempted to rid the world of evil? Might God continue to try? Consider God's inability to do so.

God regrets "smiting." Does this admission seem valid?

What are your thoughts regarding God's anger and blame?

Consider a time when regret played a part in your life. How did you act or react to either cover up or live with (or both) the regret?

Vashti and Lottie, Tamar, Deborah, Jael, and Delilah:

The women tell their own and one another's stories. What's the dynamic of a group experience/existence?

Lottie reveals Tamar's story, then takes up Vashti's tale to help reduce "triggering." How do friends aid each other in times of emotional need?

Are there elements of difficult, personal stories that are better explained by a third party?

What about group strength and compassion/protection?

Moira and Esther:

In the chapter, "A Stage Four Cancer Survivor," Moira feels that she and Esther had been destined to meet.

She asks, "Did we know each other during previous lives? Were we friends in some distant and forgotten past? Or relatives? I believe so."

Does that sense of serendipity and/or fate resonate with you?

What do long-term and short-term friendships teach us about ourselves?

How do those two differ? Is one comforting and reflective? The other challenging as well as exhilarating?

What became of Esther? How is the historical person viewed today?

Acknowledgements

The Reverend Claire Nevin-Field, the Reverend Sarah Hedgis-Kligerman, the Reverend Judith Taw Beck: three remarkable priests who challenge the status quo and helped me do so as well. Sarah's sermon on Eve and the serpent sent *Listen to Me* into early overdrive. Merry Jones who encouraged me from the beginning and posed challenging questions. And of course, Jessica Bell, Amie McCracken, and the Vine Leaves Press team who fell in love with this work and gave it a home. And Melanie Faith, who is the best editor an author could imagine. Two friends would have loved this book: Jack Comerford and the Reverend James Shannon. I miss them. My children, Cordelia Dietrich Zanger and Christian Dietrich, who have been stalwart in their support. And last, but not least, fellow author and mate Steve Zettler, who listens (endlessly) and urges me on in all my creative endeavors. Thank you all!

Also by Cordelia Frances Biddle

They Believed They Were Safe

The Martha Beale Series:
Sins of Commission
The Actress
Without Fear
Deception's Daughter
The Conjurer

Beneath the Wind

Twelve co-authored titles in the Nero Blanc mystery series

Biddle, Jackson, and a Nation in Turmoil

Saint Katharine: the Life of Katharine Drexel

www.ingramcontent.com/pod-product-compliance
Ingram Content Group UK Ltd.
Pitfield, Milton Keynes, MK11 3LW, UK
UKHW012251290726
14090UKWH00016B/591

9 783988 321275